CONFESSION AT MADDLESKIRK ABBEY

When a woman confesses to Father Will, one of the monk-constables at Maddleskirk Abbey, that she has committed murder, he can do nothing but absolve her from sin. The seal of confession is absolute but when a body is found in the nearby woodland, his moral dilemma grows. As the enquiry progresses and the clues confirm his fears that it is a murder case, Father Will must still not reveal his knowledge. Detective Chief Superintendent 'Nabber' Napier and his team have a murder to solve. The search for the killer intensifies. Questions need to be answered and confessions must be made before anybody else gets hurt.

CONFESSION AT MADDLESKIRK ABBEY

Confession At Maddleskirk Abbey

by

Nicholas Rhea

Magna Large Print Books
Long Preston, North Yorkshire,
BD23 4ND, England.

British Library Cataloguing in Publication Data.

Rhea, Nicholas
    Confession at Maddleskirk Abbey.

    A catalogue record of this book is
    available from the British Library

    ISBN   978-0-7505-4220-3

First published in Great Britain in 2015 by Robert Hale Limited

Copyright © Nicholas Rhea 2015

Cover illustration © Stephen Mulcahey by arrangement with
Arcangel Images

Published in Large Print 2016 by arrangement with
Robert Hale Limited

Magna Large Print is an imprint of Library Magna Books Ltd.

Printed and bound in Great Britain by
T.J. (International) Ltd., Cornwall, PL28 8RW

Chapter 1

'Father Will, can you do me a great favour?'

'Of course, Father Attwood. How can I help?'

'Rather unexpectedly I've been called to hospital. It follows a blood test relating to my prostate cancer. I must go to the Beach Hospital in Scarborough to be told of the findings. Six o'clock until seven. It means I can't take confessions in the abbey church this evening. Sorry about the short notice but I wondered if you could stand in for me? I've told the abbot and he sees no problem if you agree.'

'I'll be happy to do that,' said Will, smiling. 'Does it mean you'll be detained?'

'There was no suggestion of that. They didn't ask me to take my overnight things. The snag is my appointment is rather late in the day – six o'clock – which is why I can't get back in time for confessions.'

'Well, I hope it's not bad news.'

'If it was, I think I'd have been given some warning. I've got an abbey car and driver booked but I don't want him to hang about waiting. I can either get a bus back or take a taxi. Thanks for helping out, you're a good friend.'

Father John Attwood was a relatively new recruit to the Benedictine community of Maddleskirk Abbey in its beautiful setting not far from Aidensfield in the North York Moors. He had joined the monastery late in life after a career in the building industry. A widower with no family, he was a gentle person who fitted easily into the monastic routine where his knowledge of construction techniques and structural maintenance had already proved of value. He liked nothing more than fixing or repairing faults and was skilled with a range of tools. Undoubtedly he was an asset to the monastic community but, unlike Father Will Redman, he was not a member of the monk-constables, the abbey's own private police force – monkstables as they had become known. The abbot had felt that Father John was rather too old to be engaged in police work even as a gentle part-time occupation around the monastery campus. There were plenty of other activities to keep him occupied.

Father Will Redman, who was one of the monk-constables, was pleased to help his friend. Confession was one of the most important sacraments of the Church and the short notice did not present a problem. At the appointed time, Will made his way to the confessional in the abbey church. Tucked away in a quiet corner of the south transept, it was rather like a large double-sized wooden telephone kiosk with two compartments, each completely enclosed for privacy and security. He failed to notice that the wooden name-board above the penitents' door continued to display Father John Attwood's name – Father Will did not see that because he had entered the confessional via the rear door, thus avoiding the south transept. Because Father Will was not a regular hearer of confessions, he did not have his own name-board.

As he settled on the basic box-like seat, he hoped the incoming penitents would not object to this last-minute substitution. Some liked to be heard by the same confessor every time – but by his voice, which had no trace of Father John's Lancashire accent, they would quickly realize he wasn't their regular priest. They could change their minds and leave if they wished. Even though fewer people were confessing their sins in this ancient and traditional manner, confessions continued each Saturday evening between 6 p.m. and 7 p.m. in Maddleskirk Abbey Church.

In that time, a gathering of about twenty-five to thirty people could be expected to individually confess their sins in total secrecy. However, the confessional had another use. Not everyone came to confess their sins – some came for an anonymous conversation with a priest in the hope it might help them cope with some crisis or personal problem. Some lonely people came for little more than a chat and the priest was always there to help both practically and spiritually under the cloak of anonymity. Many considered this to be an additional means of helping people in need.

As Father Will prepared for his task, he wondered about the health of Father John. He had found his vocation late in life and the pair had become good friends. During one of his regular chats with Father Will, John had mentioned, somewhat casually, that as a widower with no family, he had realized that what he needed was peace, solitude and companionship in a friendly environment. A monastic community offered all that – and more. There was the added spirituality and he knew he would be cared for in the community of 120 monks, not to mention their valued role in the local community. Father John was confident he had made a wise decision and it was increasingly evident to others that he was very content with his new life.

From his hard chair in the confessional that Saturday night, Father Will Redman could not look into the south transept so he had no idea whether or not a queue had formed or how many people were waiting. He could only sit and wait for someone to enter – he couldn't go out to issue invitations! Anonymity was one of the key elements of confession.

To the right of his chair and very close to his ear was a stout wooden partition containing a small metal grille with a sliding panel. Behind that partition was the penitents' cubicle complete with kneeler, their eyes level with this sliding panel.

He could operate the slide when anyone settled at the other side. A penitent could look through the panel to see the priest's face but the separating mesh did not permit a very clear view. Likewise, he could not see the penitent's features – the darkness within the confessional added to the visitor's anonymity. During his wait, the sliding panel would be closed but he would open it when someone turned up and settled down to begin their confession. The opening of the door, which activated a low light, would alert him to an arrival.

Listening to people making their heartfelt confessions was never easy. Sometimes, people were in genuine distress at the enormity of their guilt so the act of absolution could be extremely difficult for a priest, acting as he did on God's behalf. However, it was undertaken by Catholic priests throughout the world. Even the Pope attended confession, as did priests, emperors, sovereigns, presidents and other national, political and religious leaders.

Father Will knew that this practice was something that puzzled and intrigued a large section of the general public. For Catholics, however, it was a perfectly normal part of their faith. It was constantly reinforced that the seal of confessional was absolute. No one could or should break that seal.

As Father Will waited, his long scarf-like stole, embroidered with three crosses – one at each end and one in the middle – was around his neck, hanging down with each end below waist level. The middle cross was at the back of his neck. His stole was the traditional priestly symbol of humility and service to others. As Father Will waited with his prayers and thoughts, he would do his best to provide spiritual succour to anyone in need.

Then someone arrived. He could not see who it was.

As the penitents' door opened, the electric light in that side of the confessional came on automatically but soon extinguished itself once the penitent had found the kneeler. The door closed and the rustle of clothing indicated someone had knelt down. The internal light faded although there was a dim glow of light in both cubicles. It came from the church itself, filtering through the opaque glass panels high on the outer walls of both cubicles.

The penitent took a long time to settle

down. Father Will thought it sounded like a woman with shopping bags, trying to find somewhere in the darkness to put them. When she was on the kneeler, there would be some space at either side of her, enough for a shopping bag or handbag. He waited. Eventually the silence indicated she – or perhaps he – was settled. Father Will then slid aside his panel and turned his head sideways so that his ear was close to the mesh-covered space. It was vital that he could hear the penitent's whispered confession and that no one outside could overhear it. Furthermore, he did not want to recognize his visitor.

He made the sign of the cross accompanied by the spoken words: 'In the name of the Father and of the Son and of the Holy Ghost. Amen. Please continue, take your time.'

In response a woman began to speak very softly. She had a faint but recognizable Lancashire accent and sounded middle-aged. He was sure it was not a young voice but not that of a pensioner either. Someone he knew, perhaps?

She began. 'Bless me, Father, for I have sinned. It is many, many years since my last confession. I have forgotten what to do but I have committed many venial sins...'

'That does not matter ... what does matter is that you are here now, willing to resume the practice of your faith. Do your best to recall your serious sins as you express your deep sorrow for offending God.'

'There were many trivial matters: not saying my prayers, using foul language, losing my temper, and so on.'

'They are no problem. What about mortal sins? Serious sins deliberately committed?'

There was a long silent pause and then she said, 'I'm here to confess to a mortal sin, Father.'

'Then pray, my daughter, that Almighty God will make you honest and penitent with a firm purpose of amendment. God will forgive you but only if you are truly sorry with no intention of repeating your sin—'

She interrupted him and blurted out, 'I've committed murder, Father. I've killed someone, stabbed him!' The words burst from her as if she had been keeping them hidden and was now spitting them out. She began to sob and her voice weakened as she repeated, 'I have killed, Father, please God forgive me.' And then she dissolved into a flood of tears but did not run away or leave the confessional. For a few moments Father Will remained silent. This reminded him of one of the training lessons from the seminary when all trainee priests were warned about the enormity of sins that some people might confess. All young priests and monks had been warned of the possibility that murderers, rapists or terrorists might confess some

14

dreadful actions and crimes, and that non-Catholics, old and young, might enter the confessional as some kind of sick joke.

However, the important thing was that the seal of confession was absolute even in the most extreme of cases. A priest hearing any confession must never divulge what he had been told.

As Father Will sat alone in that dark cabinet, that warning had become a reality. He could not discuss it with anyone other than the penitent and he must not make any attempt to identify her or to demand that she surrender to the police. He must not impose any condition upon her absolution, nor could he question her about the circumstances of the crime or seek the identity of the victim. He must do nothing that might lead to her identification.

So could he pronounce absolution for this woman? It all depended upon her conscience – in other words, was she genuinely sorry for what had happened? Was this a genuine confession? Or a test or joke of some kind? She was still kneeling and awaiting his reaction but would she repeat her crime? Or had she killed earlier? That was highly unlikely unless she was a serial killer. In granting her absolution, he could not require her to report her crime to the police or ask her to care for her victim's family. Although he must not come to any such agreement as

15

part of her absolution, he was able to suggest ways of easing her conscience provided they did not lead to her identity and therefore breach the seal of confession.

He waited until she had composed herself, then said in a soft voice, 'I must ask you not to agree to nor ask of me any act that would violate the seal of confession. I cannot make it a condition of absolution that you must inform the police. I cannot insist that you help any dependants who are the result of your sinfulness. You may decide to take such steps as a form of reparation but whatever decision you make, it must be entirely your own. I cannot and must not advise or compel you.'

There was no reaction. She remained in the box in total silence, so after a while he asked, 'Do you understand?'

'Yes, Father,' she whispered tearfully.

He paused again, then asked, 'I must be sure that you are truly sorry for this grievous sin.'

'I wouldn't be here otherwise, would I, Father?' And now her voice sounded stronger and her accent was emphasized. 'Of course I'm sorry ... you have not asked who I have killed ... or anything about my crime, my sin.'

'I do not want to know anything that might identify you. What you do now is your responsibility. As I have pointed out, I must not do anything or suggest anything that could break the seal of this confession.'

She burst into tears.

He continued in a soft voice, 'I need to be sure that your confession is sincere, that you are truly sorrowful and that you will never again commit such a grave sin.'

'I can promise that, Father. I am truly sorry, really I am. I cannot think what made me do it...' And she burst into another flood of tears. 'I am really, really sorry for all this.'

Her sobs intensified and he felt sure they could be heard by the others queuing in the transept.

'I shall grant absolution. Can you hear me?'

'I can,' she whispered in a husky voice.

Making the sign of the cross in front of her secret and tearful face behind the mesh, he pronounced the words of absolution:

'In the name of the Father and of the Son and of the Holy Ghost, Almighty God now absolves you from your sin. Go in peace to love and serve the Lord. Amen. Now you may go and God be with you.'

There was a rustling sound as she rose to her feet. The light in her cubicle switched itself on as he was closing the small partition. Then she departed with the curious words, 'And I know what you did, Father. Remember that. I know *your* secret, *your* sin.'

Then she was gone. The light went out and the door closed behind her. Father Will sat in stunned silence awaiting the next penitent. He was alone for just a few minutes before the next one arrived but he could not forget that woman's parting words.

But could he or should he ignore them?

Chapter 2

In his capacity as security advisor to Maddleskirk Abbey, retired Inspector Nick Rhea, the former village constable of nearby Aidensfield, paid regular visits to the abbey. Each Monday he spent half an hour or so with the monkstables. Sometimes he would analyze reported incidents to ensure they had been correctly dealt with, or he may give advice on matters arising from those discussions. Those Monday morning sessions were always eagerly awaited as the monks gradually developed a deeper understanding of their police role.

Nick also arranged bi-monthly meetings to consider changes or improvements. Overall, of course, he was expected to advise on any major problem or to give spontaneous advice in phone calls to his home. Although he had retired from the police in the rank of inspector, he found his new role interesting and stimulating – and he was paid a small but useful retainer.

In creating this small private police force, he'd had help from retired police sergeant Oscar Blaketon and ex-PC Alf Ventress of Ashfordly, who were always keen to be involved. The tiny police force comprised a highly effective unit of eight monks plus their leader, Prior Tuck of Maddleskirk Abbey. The monkstables dealt with a wide range of internal problems such as bad car parking, dropped litter and unruly behaviour, often by trespassers, whilst criminal or serious matters remained the responsibility of the North Yorkshire Police.

Every day, each monkstable performed an eight-hour shift patrolling in police uniform within the spacious estate that comprised Maddleskirk Abbey and College. The rest of their time was devoted to their monastic calling. On occasions, one or more monkstables might be directed to one of the external properties that came within the abbey's jurisdiction, such as a school or parish.

In addition, and upon request, they could be seconded temporarily to other local abbeys or convents such as Ampleforth, Stanbrook or the Bar Convent in York. The likelihood of a female monkstable being recruited had not been overlooked – a nun-stable perhaps? That idea was awaiting development and was proving of interest to the local convents and indeed the abbeys.

Under the capable leadership of Prior Tuck, himself a former police officer, the monkstables were doing a good job – there was less litter around the campus, there had been a reduction in bad language and noisy behaviour, and there was an awareness of the need for good parking along with more considerate driving and cycling. People seemed to take more care when walking through the grounds, even collecting litter they had found, to then drop it in a waste bin.

One surprising bonus was that a lot of found property had been restored to its owners and the uniformed monkstables were also proving very knowledgeable guides to the increasing numbers of daily tourists or those on retreat. They could even perform car-parking duties during major events at the abbey. There was no doubt the monkstables, in their smart black uniforms and white helmets, were proving extremely effective. Black was the colour of the habits worn by the Benedictines; most police uniforms were a very dark navy blue.

On that Monday morning in September Nick walked from his home to the abbey, a journey of some ten minutes. As he strode along he was aware of a military helicopter flying down the valley; it was using a designated route that avoided built-up areas. Monday was when the army cadet corps was on parade to deal with staged incidents, often arranged by incoming professional soldiers of all ranks. The 'copter would land on the helipad within the grounds and would be used in today's training of the corps.

Helicopters from both military and private sources were a regular sight around the college. Even the Archbishop of Canterbury had once arrived by helicopter, sparking a rumour that he was about to convert to Catholicism and join the Benedictines.

With the autumn foliage showing its seasonal colours, Nick was heading for the cop shop within the main building. It had formerly been the abbey and college shop, selling everything from sweets to fashionable clothes. When the shop had transferred to larger premises, the old tuck shop had found a new role as the abbey's own dedicated police station. Inevitably, it became known as the cop shop. During opening hours it was staffed by one of the monk-constables whilst a couple of the others would be patrolling the huge site in between their monastic duties.

With its blue light above the entrance, the cop shop had all the appearances of a small busy police station, which in fact it was. On office duty that day was Father Will Redman, a small studious man in his early fifties with thick spectacles and an amazing knowledge of monastic history and culture. His understanding of computers had been a wonderful bonus to the monkstables and through his technical knowledge the cop shop was now linked to the control room at the county police headquarters and also the local police station at Ashfordly. Under Father Will's guidance, security cameras had been installed in selected areas of the abbey and college, both internally and externally. After each tour of duty, the monkstables entered their daily records in the cop shop computer system, an ideal means of maintaining up-to-date information about all the events and occurrences in and around Maddleskirk Abbey and College.

'Ah, Nick, good morning,' greeted Father Will. 'Nothing much to report so far today and it's been very quiet overnight.'

'Is anything happening on the site that we should know about?'

'I have to say that our systems are functioning well and the important thing is that the staff and visitors know that we're here if we're needed. Outside, there is the monthly corps exercise and parade by the college students but they look after themselves. Our patrols will pay visits from time to time, just to show a presence!'

'That's how it should be. So is the cop shop keeping busy?'

'Surprisingly so. We're obviously fulfilling a need. People – visitors and staff – come regularly for all sorts of reasons which is most gratifying. Now, Nick, whilst we are alone, I have something to tell you...'

Father Will wanted to discuss Father John's visit to hospital because he had not yet returned, but at that moment the door opened and in strode Barnaby Crabstaff accompanied by a whiff of heavy sweat and other indefinable but not very pleasant odours.

'Ah, Constable Rhea,' he panted. 'I saw you heading this way as I was coming here so because I wanted a chat to tell you something important I came right here right away right now so as to catch you before you left and here you are...'

'So I am, Barnaby. Is there something you want?'

'I was coming to the cop shop to report this but when I saw you I thought you might know what to do and if you'd not been here then I would have spoken to this officer standing here but because you are here, I may as well mention it to you. Or to both of you.'

'I think I know what you mean,' Nick responded after deciphering Barnaby's speech. 'How can we help?'

'I think there's a body up there in Ashwell Priory woods...' He lapsed into a whisper as he pointed vaguely to somewhere outside. 'Or he could be just asleep.'

'A body?' asked Father Will with a clear look of horror on his face. Nick did not miss his expression – it reminded him of a child's guilt when a personal secret has been discovered. Did Father Will know something about this? Had it already been reported?

'It's a man and he's not moving. He's cold and stiff but if he's been sleeping outside on a chilly night like last night then he would be cold so perhaps he's not very dead...'

'Who is it, Barnaby? Any idea?'

'Sorry, no, Mr Rhea, not a clue. Never seen him before.'

'Does anyone else know about this?'

'I think not, Mr Rhea, they'd never go walking where he is lying, it's off the footpath and deep among the rocks and trees, so it is, off the beaten track as they say but I go there quite a lot, looking for rare birds which is why I was there and why I found him, if you understand. I was not poaching, Mr Rhea, or anything like that...'

'All right, Barnaby, you'd better show us,' suggested Nick. 'Do you want to come with me, Father Will? As a monkstable of this abbey this might be our responsibility even if he's not on abbey land, or shall I find someone else?'

'Can you find someone else?' His voice quivered slightly. 'I'll stay and look after the office. I might be needed here. Monkstable Dale is patrolling somewhere around the abbey, probably looking in on the corps parades, so I'll call him on his mobile. He should go with you.'

24

'You're right, he should.'

They waited as Father Will phoned Monk-stable Dale. Nick attempted to coax more of the story from Barnaby whilst doing his best not to suggest in any way that he was responsible.

Nick was well acquainted with Barnaby and knew that the poor fellow had an enormous guilt complex. However, from what he said, it seemed he'd been bird watching in Ashwell Priory woods earlier that morning when he'd stumbled across the man lying on the ground. He was among trees some distance from the footpath in an isolated location. That little-used path twisted up the hillside before arriving at St Valentine's Well, now regarded as a wishing well but in reality a pond about the size of a tennis court. It was not usual to find such a pond or well on a hilltop but this was due to the many springs in the area, some overflowing at high altitude from the huge water-filled caverns underground. This locality was almost a mile from the abbey whilst being deep within Nick's recently inherited Ashwell Priory woodland. The casualty was therefore on Nick's property. But he said nothing about that at this stage.

As Barnaby's tale unfolded under gentle questioning, he suggested the man would be difficult to find because he was lying in thick undergrowth, adding that he was not dressed in hiking gear but wore a dark green T-shirt, blue jeans and white canvas plimsolls. He said the man had white skin, dark hair and was about thirty years old. Barnaby had not noticed a rucksack nearby, neither had he seen a tent in the woods – but as he said he had visited only a very small part of the entire woodland, which was rather isolated. Nick wondered whether he should call a doctor or even the county police, but decided it would be wise to first establish the true situation. Barnaby's assessment might be faulty – the fellow might have been lying asleep or hiding in the hope of spotting a rare bird. Nick did not wish to cause undue alarm or unnecessary work by rushing headlong into the situation. A cautious approach was needed.

'Barnaby, can we be sure this is a body? Could it be somebody asleep?'

'First I thought he was asleep, Mr Rhea, and I tried to wake him to ask if he was all right but his cheek was cold and stiff so now I think he's dead, so I do.'

'Anything else? Did you notice anything else?'

'A spot or two of blood near his head. Among the leaves. I never touched that, I swear.'

'Blood? Where would it have come from? Any idea?'

'It was near his head, on some leaves. I saw it. I never touched it, and I never did touch

26

him either, so help me...'

'I know you didn't, Barnaby. You've done the right thing by telling us about it. So will you show us where he is?'

The shock of the discovery must have alarmed poor Barnaby so it was rather surprising that he had responded by informing the police. It reminded Nick of the help Barnaby had given when young Simon Houghton had been trapped in the ruins of Ashwell Priory. Maybe in his maturity he was mellowing and coming to trust the police? Nick hoped so – Barnaby was good-hearted, if devious to a degree, but always nervous in the presence of police officers and priests.

'Yes, I can take you there.' And at that opportune moment, Father Alban Dale arrived. Tall, slim, fair-haired and in his forties, he was often called Allan after the Robin Hood character of Allan a' Dale. One of his great ambitions was to visit every Marian shrine in the world, but this ancient pilgrimage site and its small well was dedicated to St Valentine so he hadn't included that in his itinerary. Nonetheless, he had often visited the holy well for no other reason than it had once been the venue for pilgrimages. Equipped with portable radio sets, Father Alban, Barnaby and Nick used an abbey van to speed through the grounds towards Ashwell Priory woods.

Father Alban parked near the old barns.

They walked the final quarter of a mile and it took about twenty minutes to clamber up the steep hillside path as it snaked through the trees. Near the summit, Barnaby veered off the path to trudge through knee-deep undergrowth and bracken towards a patch of beech trees growing among very large boulders.

'He's over there,' whispered Barnaby, pointing ahead towards the base of a very high cliff. 'That's where he was when I left...'

'Well, I hope he's not there now,' Nick commented. 'I hope he's alive and he's woken up to continue his walk or whatever he came to do.'

But the man was there; white-faced, still and deathly, just as Barnaby had described. He was lying face up beneath the canopy of beeches as if they formed his final resting place. The eight tall trees had the appearance of an ancient temple with the deceased in the centre awaiting his spiritual fate. To their immediate left was the high cliff of local limestone. Had he fallen from there? Or jumped? Or staggered here before collapsing? He seemed rather too far from the cliff face to have fallen. With white skin, he was of a fairly tall height with dark hair and he appeared to be in his thirties, just as Barnaby had said. He was wearing a dark green T-shirt, blue jeans and white canvas plimsolls. His eyes were closed and there did not seem to be any injuries on his body, or any personal belongings nearby, such as a rucksack. There was not even a watch on his wrist.

Nick shouted a loud 'Hello' to test for a reaction, but there was none. Aware that one should never unnecessarily pollute a crime scene, Nick stood back from the body and from a distance surveyed the surroundings to acquire a clear mental memory of those moments. He took several photographs with his mobile phone.

In spite of his caution, however, he must ascertain whether or not the man was dead. As the others stood at a discreet distance, Nick approached with care, noting his route for future reference so that CID would step into the same footmarks. Then he reached down and touched the man's cheek. It was stone cold and wax-like; he was unsure whether rigor mortis had set in.

If it had, it could have disappeared by now and there was no way of determining whether this man had been subjected to it. Nick then raised one of the man's eyelids – the eye was dead and dull with no sign of life. There was no pulse either, and no heartbeat. From where Nick was operating he could not see any sign of blood but there was ample evidence that they now had a corpse – with no indication of how or when he had arrived, who he was or what had caused his death. The absence of the smell of death and the

lack of visible signs of decomposition suggested the body had arrived fairly recently,
probably within the last day or two.

'Where did you see the blood? I haven't
found any,' Nick asked Barnaby.

'Below his head. You need to go over there,
Mr Rhea: you can see better from that bump
in the ground. Look under his head ... I
thought the ground looked soaked in blood
under his head ... or it might have been
something else. You can never tell ... animal
blood, mebbe. Coloured leaves.'

Nick went to the place he indicated, took
a close look without moving the body and
then agreed with him.

'Yes, from here it looks like blood,
Barnaby. From the back of his head. Maybe
a head injury when he fell? Do you think he
might have fallen off that high cliff while
bird watching?'

'He could have done that, Mr Rhea, but
he has no binoculars or camera. Nothing at
all by the look of things. He could have
taken a nasty tumble off that cliff top but I
never saw it happen, so I did not.'

'Did you hear a shout? A commotion of
any kind?'

'Not a thing, Mr Rhea. All was quiet when
I got here this morning, except those helicopters ... going to the college. They scare
the birds, so they do.'

'What time would that be?'

30

'Not too early, half eight or so. Nine o'clockish maybe.'

'Right. So any sounds of gunshots? Shouting? Screaming? Cries for help? Indications of trouble of any kind? This morning or any other time?'

'No, Mr Rhea, nothing but the sounds of birds in the trees. Singing as if it was springtime.'

'Right. So in those moments just before you found him, did you notice anything that might have been out of the ordinary? Loud voices, other people in the wood, arguments, someone running away, a car or motorbike on the road below ... anything at all that's not usual? Not just today but recently.'

'No, not a thing, Mr Rhea, it's been as silent as the grave for weeks.'

'And just to confirm things, we don't know who he is or where he's come from.'

'To be sure we don't, Mr Rhea. I don't know him. I've never seen him before, so I have not. It's all very puzzling.'

Nick decided not to search the victim's pockets and the nearby ground for anything that might lead to his identification – almost certainly he would have credit cards, cash, handkerchief and probably some means of identification but it was not the job of this small team or any of the monkstables.

That was the task of the incoming detectives, as Nick explained to Barnaby and

Father Alban.

'Well, whatever's happened, it's a suspicious death,' Nick confirmed. 'It needs to be investigated but not by us. We must call in CID. I'll get Father Will to contact the control room at police headquarters to set things in motion. We need a doctor to certify death but not the cause of death, then we'll have to bring in a forensic pathologist. Scenes of Crime will examine the scene before the body is removed.'

'So there's nothing we can do for him, is there?' asked Father Alban.

'Not to save his life, no. It's too late for that. I'm not a doctor but I know a dead body when I see one.'

Father Alban made the sign of the cross and lowered his head to whisper some short prayers, so Barnaby and Nick lapsed into a respectful silence and stood very still with their heads bowed.

When he had finished, Father Alban asked, 'You think he's been attacked, Nick? That blood...'

'At this stage, Father, it looks very likely. Perhaps a blow to the head but we can't rule out an accident of some kind. Even if he fell off that cliff, he might have been pushed. The nature of his head wound should reveal something. What we need to do – the monkstables, that is – is to find out who he is and where he's come from.'

'Could he have been at The Grange?' asked Father Alban. 'On one of the residential retreats? I've known some take long walks in the woods around here, and others have visited the former holy well up there among the trees, a sort of miniature pilgrimage. It's on modern maps and the footpath up to it is clearly in regular use.'

'I'll make sure enquiries are made at The Grange, Father. Thanks for that.'

'So do we need an ambulance, Nick? Shall I call ours from the infirmary? Or would the air ambulance be better here?'

'Neither! Ambulances are for saving life, not for carrying dead people around. Besides, there's nowhere nearby for a helicopter to land. In any case he can't be moved until the doctor and a forensic pathologist have examined him.'

'That's the sort of thing I keep forgetting!'

'Not to worry. Once we hand responsibility to the county constabulary, they will see to all the necessary follow-up action. Because the scene must be examined as a possible crime scene, we mustn't attempt to move the body or disturb anything.'

'So we'll not be needed here any more then?'

'The monkstables will be expected to help with local enquiries but this is too serious for us to deal with. We should remain here to protect the scene until the CID arrive;

they'll want to talk to us first.'

'You mean me as well, Mr Rhea?' asked Barnaby.

'You especially!' said Nick.

'I didn't realize that finding a body involved so much, so I did not.'

Nick radioed Father Will in the cop shop and explained the situation, requesting a doctor and the county CID along with a forensic pathologist, the Scenes of Crime team, official photographer and a pair of uniform constables to take over the guarding of the scene for as long as necessary. That transferred the incident from the hands of the monkstables even though Nick, Father Alban and Barnaby remained to relate their stories to the incoming CID.

After what seemed a long time Monkstable Dale's mobile produced a voice asking for directions and there was an audible sense of relief that assistance was en route even though there was no urgency to save life. After a few minutes, several vehicles could be heard as they eased to a halt on the access road below the main body of woodland but it required a few more location directions to establish precisely where to find the body. Father Alban said he would go down to guide them to the scene.

'You won't need me now, Mr Rhea.' Barnaby prepared to leave.

'You'd better stay a while, Barnaby, CID will want to talk to you.' Nick reminded him of the reasons. 'If you leave, they'll simply come to find you.'

'What can I say to them, Mr Rhea?' he asked with genuine concern.

'Just tell them what you told me.' Nick tried to reassure the little fellow, conscious of his fear of police officers. 'You've nothing to be scared of, Barnaby. Because you found the body, you're a very important witness.'

'If you say so, Mr Rhea. They won't think I did it, will they?'

'Not if you stay here with me. But they might think that if you go away.'

'Then I'll stay.'

First to arrive was Detective Sergeant Jim Sullivan in whose local area of responsibility the body lay. Led by Father Alban, he was closely followed by the Scenes of Crime team, police photographers, a doctor and a forensic pathologist.

All had apparently assembled somewhere nearby to be sure all reached the correct place.

'We meet again, Nick,' said Sullivan. 'I thought this was miles from murder and mayhem! First a dead man in the coffin in the crypt, now a man lying in a remote area of woodland. Show me the body and tell me what you know, then I'll start the interviews whilst the experts do their stuff. So who is

35

this chap? Any ideas, anyone?'

'No idea,' said Barnaby, and the others echoed his words.

'He's not a local then?'

'I've never seen him around,' said Nick.

'I've never seen him around,' echoed Barnaby.

And so began the formal examination of the corpse, with the doctor pronouncing him dead but not attempting to determine the cause. That was not his job. Then the forensic pathologist began his preliminary but detailed examination of both the body and the nearby woodland. Under his direction, the Scenes of Crime team began their search of the area they had already cordoned off with bright yellow tape, albeit with the body in situ. They would be looking for evidence among the undergrowth, even a weapon of some kind or something discarded by the killer or killers. The body remained exactly where it was until all the experts felt it and its clothing could be examined and searched, in an attempt to find documents or evidence of identity. A much more detailed scientific search of the body and its clothing would be made in the forensic laboratory but the detectives needed a starting point before the body was removed.

As the scientists and Scenes of Crime experts worked, Detective Sergeant Sullivan took Barnaby to one side.

'So, Barnaby,' he said, smiling, 'what can you tell me about all this?'

'Nothing, sir.'

'There's no need to call me sir. I'm a sergeant. Detective sergeant actually.'

'Right, sir, I understand.'

'Tell me how you found this man. Show me where you were when you first saw him, and then, once you had found him, tell me what you did next. Take your time, Barnaby, you're not in any kind of bother. We just need to know all about it. As much as you can tell us. The more you can tell us, the easier it will be for us all.'

'I see, sir, so I do,' and he took a deep breath.

He then launched into a rambling account of how he had been bird watching in the woods that morning when he had noticed the man lying there, at first thinking he was asleep. But after a time the man had not moved and so Barnaby had approached him to see if he was all right, then realized he was dead. He'd walked around to look at him from a distance, which was when he'd noticed the blood beneath his head.

'Scenes of Crime will want to look at your boots, Barnaby, to take scrapings and perhaps imprints of their soles, just to see whether anyone else had been attending the body before you found him. We don't suspect you, Barnaby, but we are trying to prove that you are innocent; we want to eliminate you from our enquiries.'

'If you say so, sir.'

'So before you found the body, did you see or hear anybody else in these woods this morning?'

'No, sir, not a soul. Honest, nobody.'

'And last night? Or yesterday?'

'I wasn't here then, sir, not yesterday. I was working over at Ploatby, helping with the harvest.'

'Ah, which farm?'

'Throstle Nest, sir. Mr Hendry's place.'

'So when was the previous time you were here?'

'Oh, it would be some weeks ago, sir.'

'Obviously before this man arrived?'

'It must have been, I never saw him until this morning, lying where he is now.'

'That agrees with what I think. I'd hazard a guess that he's been here only for a day or two at the most. There's nothing to indicate how he got here unless he fell or jumped off that cliff. Or was pushed. Thanks for your help, Barnaby. Will you be around if we want a chat?'

'I'm here for another few days. I sleep in the old barns just down the road then I'll be moving, I don't know where. Helping with a harvest. Not far away.'

'Will anyone know where to find you?'

'Mr Greengrass might.'

'Claude Jeremiah lives at Aidensfield,' Nick told the detective. 'I know him well enough.'

'Thanks. Now when our officers have finished their initial examination, we'll transfer the body into a mortuary for a more detailed scientific examination. It might take some time. You can all leave if you wish.'

'Can I stay to see what goes on?' Barnaby asked. 'In all my born days, I've never seen this sort of thing, so I have not.'

'Yes, of course,' responded Sullivan, much to everyone's surprise. 'We might want more help from you as we go along, so stay as long as you want but don't stray into that area inside our yellow tape.'

'No, sir, I won't, I promise I won't. Thank you for letting me stay, I've never seen such a thing in my life, never.'

With Sullivan's consent, everyone remained as a tight little bunch of observers as the meticulous work proceeded. It was a splendid display of police work that benefited the monkstables watching. Sadly, they could not all be there to witness the work at a crime scene but Father Alban said he would relate his experiences to his colleagues.

The examination and ground search of the area began, including the stately beech trees and the top of the small cliff that overlooked the death scene. The official photographer recorded everything including the removal of soil samples and the collection of leaf-mould for forensic analysis. In all, the examination continued for about two hours. It was fortunate that DS Sullivan provided a running commentary to explain what was going on, and why such a detailed examination was necessary.

'Detective Chief Superintendent Napier is on his way,' he told them after taking a call on his mobile. 'He'll want to examine both the scene and the body in situ. There's little more we can do until he arrives and I'm sure he'll call out the full murder team. The stretcher is on its way and once Mr Napier has viewed the body, it will be placed in a mortuary vehicle to be taken to Middlesbrough for a forensic post-mortem.'

There was a brief lapse of activity, then everything changed. Puffing through the undergrowth with his large size and famous big feet trampling shrubs and crushing plants, Detective Chief Superintendent Roderick (Nabber) Napier arrived with Detective Inspector Brian Lindsey at his side. They were quickly followed by the stretcher party consisting of four powerful young policemen, and after they had placed the stretcher close to the body, the pathologist, along with Napier and Lindsey, came for a closer look. No one said anything as the party toured the area around the corpse, sometimes checking the ground before standing on it and sometimes moving aside ferns and other undergrowth.

'Where's the famous wishing well in relation to this site?' Napier asked of anyone who might be listening.

Nick pointed through the trees to a higher site. 'A five-minute climb up there, Mr Napier,' he said. 'There's a reasonable foot-path. It's a pond rather than a mere well or spring.'

'On a hilltop?'

'That's right.' Nick gave him a brief ex-planation.

'Thanks, we learn something every day. We'll need a look up there. A pond is a good place for hiding weapons and other evidence. So where's the blood you mentioned?' asked Napier of Sullivan, without bothering with polite formalities. 'Show me.'

As the body's head was carefully elevated, Napier looked at the back of the victim's head.

'There's a lot of blood on the ground. Dead people don't generally bleed but with this chap lying like this with his head lower than his carcase, I'd say much of it has drained away rather than being pumped out with his heartbeats. It looks like a deep puncture wound to me,' Napier told Detective Ser-geant Sullivan. 'In the back of the neck. A deep round hole. Is it a bullet wound? Have you found a discarded firearm? Handgun, I'd guess. Large calibre if the size of that wound is anything to go by. Or discarded bullet cases? This undergrowth is dense enough to conceal a lot of stuff. Or is this a dagger wound? Bayonet even? Recently there has been a spate of stiletto wounds in some parts of the country. Drugs barons at war and still using stilettos. A sort of trademark ... they're available if you know where to look. So we must find out more about this chap. We need to be sure who he is and how he died, and we need to find the weapon. I don't think he died in a fall; those wounds suggest otherwise. I reckon he was dead before he landed at the bottom of that cliff.'

'We searched the undergrowth but found nothing.'

'So there's nothing to show who he is or where he's from?'

'No, boss. Not a thing.'

'Right, listen hard. I believe this is a high-priority case; it smacks of a very professional killing. When we've finished searching the scene, the next thing is to get this chap into the blood wagon and off to his post-mortem. It's murder, Sergeant. No doubt about it. Probably killed up there and thrown off the cliff. Not the sort of killing you'd expect in such a quiet, remote place. If you want to know what I really think, I'd say this has all the hallmarks of a drugs-related gangland execution.'

Chapter 3

The unaccustomed activity in the college corridors, abbey precincts and now the woodland across the valley made Father Will feel very isolated in the cop shop. He needed something to take his mind off the woman's confession, but he couldn't stop wondering whether it had any connection with the body in the wood.

And then there had been another dimension, not part of that woman's confession. She had whispered that she knew his secret. Except it wasn't *his* secret – obviously she thought she was speaking to Father Attwood. So who was she to know Father John's secret? That thought reminded him that Father John had not yet returned from hospital, neither had there been any news about him. He had not attended any abbey functions or meals since Saturday and no one had mentioned him or seemed particularly concerned. Had he been detained in hospital? Surely someone would know? The abbot or prior probably. He decided to try and find out.

He was aware that the woman's confession would trouble him for the rest of his life. There was no one with whom he could discuss it, share it or from whom he could seek advice. In retrospect, he believed he had done everything he could and should have done. He had followed the rules in a difficult situation. And because the woman had expressed her contrition, he'd had no option but to absolve her – there was nothing else he could have done.

Was her victim that man in the woods? But he must not think like that ... she had confessed and it was all over. Finished. Completely finished. He must forget she had ever spoken to him, that she had ever confessed such a crime. But had she spoken the entire truth? She said she'd stabbed someone but suppose she had been *planning* to kill someone?

Could he have prevented that? He told himself once again that it was all over now. Forever.

But what about her parting comment? That had *not* been part of her confession, she had spoken the words *after* absolution, and so he felt he could question their meaning. And the logical thing was to ask Father John when he returned because the parting comment had been directed at him! It was very odd there had been no word either from him or the hospital. Surely the hospital had rung? Perhaps they'd contacted the abbot's secretary? Maybe someone at reception had taken the call without thinking to inform the community? That was highly likely in a place as busy and as large as Maddleskirk Abbey and College and in any case, there was no requirement that Father Will or any of the other monks should be made aware of Father Attwood's medical condition. With 120 monks in the monastery, one person could not know everything about each of them.

He began to wonder how he could trace the woman to ask about her knowledge of Father Attwood's secret. Might she know where he was now? There was no need to tell anyone about his plan; he could do it quietly.

But first he had to check the whereabouts of Father John. He rang the prior's secretary, who said the prior had been told of the death in the wood and was already in the Postgate Room preparing it for the monkstables' inevitable role in the investigation. Will rang the prior on an internal line.

'Tuck,' responded the cheerful voice.

'Father Will Redman,' he announced, there being two Father Wills in the monastery, both monkstables. 'I'm in the cop shop, Father Prior. I've heard about the body in the wood, so I'm anxious to find out what happened to Father John after he was admitted to hospital.'

'That's worrying me too,' responded the prior. 'At my meeting with Father Abbot this morning, the matter of Father John was raised. No one has heard from him since Saturday night, when I believe you stood in for him at confessions.'

'Yes, I did.'

'I've checked at this end – certainly he was delivered to Scarborough Beach Hospital by our driver. He saw Father John being escorted away by a woman. The driver understood Father John was being shown to a specialist unit. It was to do with his prostate cancer – something had shown up in the analysis of a blood sample.'

'So we know he got there. Has anyone rung the hospital to enquire about him?'

'Yes, I did, but not until this morning. And there's the problem. They've no record of him being there. The computers don't record him being admitted as a patient on Saturday. In short, Father Will, they deny knowing anything about him or his whereabouts.'

'That's impossible! Or inefficient! We know he got there!'

'Yes, I told them that and then I asked for a physical check – a body search in other words – of all the wards, corridors, side wards, waiting rooms, everywhere. That is underway as we speak. I'm awaiting a return call – my secretary knows where to find me.'

'It's a relief to know things are moving. I must say it's odd he should vanish just before that body was found...'

'He arrived at the hospital long before the

body was found, Father Will. He went on Saturday evening and the body wasn't found until this morning.'

'But we don't know *when* the man was killed, do we?' persisted Will.

'We don't but I hardly think it was the work of a monk!'

'I'm not suggesting he committed the murder, Father Prior, I am just getting the sequence of events straightened out in my head. I stood in for him during the confessions at six on Saturday evening whilst he went off to hospital. Since then, nothing! Except a murder. I must say I find that very worrying, very odd indeed.'

'Let's not read too much into this. Clearly there are matters to be clarified. Surely he must be in that hospital even if it claims to have no record of him. I trust they will carry out a full and proper search, not just relying on computers and files. They need to look into every likely hiding place ... this is awful ... truly awful.'

'Didn't the hospital telephone him to ask him to attend? Rather urgently?'

'That's what I understand, Father Will. I pray he is still there under care even if he is lying on a trolley in a corridor.'

'Let's hope so.'

And so Father Will returned to his duties in the cop shop, his mind in further turmoil. The problem was that Father Will, a close friend of John, knew that John *did* have a very, very dark secret. But how could that woman have known?

Nick, Barnaby and Father Alban were preparing to leave the scene of the death when Detective Chief Superintendent Napier hailed them.

'Before you go,' he shouted, 'can one of you pave the way for us to use the theatre again? The one we used last time. It will be our incident room. The monkstables will be using the Postgate Room, it's already being set up for them.'

'I'll let the abbot know what's happened,' said Father Alban. 'I'm sure there'll be no objection.'

'There is one matter to remember, I recall it from last time I was here. This woodland does not belong to the abbey or college, so the murder has not been committed on their property. For that reason, the abbey might not want us using their premises. Tell the abbot not to be afraid to say no. If necessary, I'm prepared to hire a suitable room locally. Funds are available.'

'I don't think there'll be a problem,' Father Alban assured him. 'The crime scene is near enough to be of concern to the staff and monks. I'd say the abbot will do all in his power to help. I'll inform him immediately.'

'So who owns this woodland? Didn't you

tell me, Nick, last time we were here, that you'd inherited land and property hereabouts?'

'That's right, it belongs to me now. The necessary paperwork was recently completed. If I had a building that you could use, I'd willingly let you do so but my old stables are no good. There's no power, water or security. No doors either!'

'Fair enough. So have you plans for the property?' asked Napier.

'Nothing at the moment. I'm merely trying to come to terms with my inheritance. I don't even know my benefactors. I've never heard of them or met them but understand they are relations from centuries ago. Some legal wizard traced their links to me. I'm honest when I say I have no idea what to do with my land.'

'I hope it doesn't become a burden.'

'I'll consider very carefully anything that's associated with it,' Nick assured him. 'And now we must leave. We don't want to hinder your work.'

'I'll need help from your fellow monkstables, Father Alban. The victim might be associated with the college or abbey, or could even be from the local district. Perhaps you could alert the abbot and then assemble all the monkstables so I can address them before I brief my own teams? They're not all here yet.'

'No problem.'

'It'll take some time for my detectives to assemble; some are travelling long distances. North Yorkshire's a big place! In the meantime, your monkstables can begin: they'll be ideal for starting and following up local enquiries.'

'We'd be delighted to help,' said Father Alban.

Barnaby indicated he would not be accompanying the others back to the cop shop. He had a business meeting with Claude Jeremiah Greengrass and so Father Alban drove the van back to base with Nick as sole passenger. They went immediately to the cop shop where Father Will Redman looked anxious and preoccupied.

'Well?' he asked with just a hint of impatience. 'What's the latest?'

'It's got all the hallmarks of a murder,' Nick told him. 'A man has been found dead at the foot of a cliff in Ashwell Priory woods apparently with stab wounds. He's not far from the former holy well. Some local CID teams are there now, others are expected soon. Once they've completed their examination of the scene and the body, the victim will be taken away for a post-mortem. Once again, they'd like to establish their murder/incident room in St Alban's Lecture Theatre. We'll be in the Postgate Room.'

'That shouldn't be a problem.' Will

produced a weak smile. 'So how was the murder committed? You mentioned stab wounds?'

'It's not absolutely certain until the PM result but it looks like a deep wound in the neck at the lower part of the head at the rear. Mr Napier talked of gang warfare involving drugs; he reckons the wound could be a stab wound, a sort of criminal trademark.'

'In this locality? Surely those are urban crimes...'

'Not any more!'

'When did it happen?'

'We're not sure but the body looks fairly fresh. Yesterday, perhaps, or two days ago, but probably not earlier. There's no decomposition.'

'St Alban's is not being used at the moment and it would be very convenient for Mr Napier and his officers. The abbot will surely agree. So is there any hint of the victim's identity or whether he is linked to the abbey or college?'

'We know nothing at the moment except it's a white male probably in his thirties,' replied Nick. 'All his personal belongings have been removed – that's another indication of a skilled criminal at work.'

'Oh dear, this sounds ominous. Once we have the abbot's consent for use of St Alban's, the monkstables can help to set it up. And we shall use the Postgate Room as our own base.'

'That will be fine,' Nick agreed. 'Mr Napier wants us to carry out local enquiries and we'll be briefed very soon.'

'I think we should update Prior Tuck.' Father Will spoke softly. 'He's been notified of the death and is already preparing the Postgate Room for us.'

'I'll contact him there – I need to explain the latest about Father John, and you should all know too.'

Everyone fell silent as Father Will explained the mystery surrounding Father John Attwood's apparent disappearance, although he gave no hint that the missing monk had a secret. 'We're awaiting the result of a search of the entire hospital; he must be there somewhere.'

'You'll keep us informed?'

'Of course.'

'Meanwhile, it's time for our briefing,' announced Father Alban.

When most of the monkstables had assembled in the Postgate Room, the door burst open and in strode the massive bulk of Detective Chief Superintendent Roderick Seymour Napier. At about six feet six inches tall and of proportionate width due to his weight of seventeen or eighteen stone, his renowned feet, large and wide apart at the toes like the points of a clock showing ten minutes to two, carried him forward. As he waddled into the room, a waitress arrived and placed some coffee percolators on the table then departed. Napier's eyes focused on Father Alban as he said, 'Good morning, Reverend Constable. So we meet again. Is your boss here?'

'Prior Tuck's on his way but right now he's briefing the abbot.'

'You don't waste time, I'll grant you that! I thought I'd come here to formally appoint your monkstables to my team whilst explaining what we know already,' he said. 'Now, is that a coffee pot I see before me? I could murder a cup of hot strong coffee. We can do that while we wait for the others.'

As more monkstables appeared in their smart police uniforms, a few detectives joined them, filling their cups and selecting chocolate biscuits, but there was no discussion about the murder in the woods. That would come later. The chatter was small talk about the weather, the influx of visitors over the summer months and the quieter times that had followed. Several referred to the ongoing building work at the far side of the abbey estate where new buildings – accommodation blocks, classrooms, laboratories and yet another library – were under construction. This work brought in hundreds of workers from all over Britain, some only on a very temporary basis even as short as one day, and others with more permanent posts.

It meant the normally peaceful grounds of the abbey and college were now having to tolerate the non-stop buzz of machinery and the constant movement of personnel and vehicles. And a veritable host of murder suspects.

Father Will did not attend the briefing because it was felt he should not leave the cop shop unattended. With the college busy with its autumn term, all the monks were settling down to their usual routine. Their summer retreats were over although some had been scheduled for autumn; all had had their holidays away from the monastery and all would be committed to their own individual tasks over the coming months. Among the commitments to be accommodated within their busy lives were the supervision of pilgrimages, spirituality courses, meditation sessions, lectures on a variety of Catholic teachings and those of other faiths along with some practical sessions such as a wine tasting, liturgical matters, a motor mechanics course, an art class, a computer seminar and the history of Easter in England. Christmas, one of their busiest times of the year, also lay ahead. As always, the monks would be fully occupied over and above the practice of their personal daily office and attendance at Mass. And there was always the need to rehearse their spiritual singing – in fact, they had just released a CD of Gregorian chants.

Then Prior Tuck arrived.

'Now then, Friar Tuck,' boomed Napier with a mischievous glint in his eyes. 'Been to consult Robin Hood, have you?'

'Yes, I got him sorted out, then I sharpened his arrows but suggested he should be careful not to shoot himself in the foot,' said Prior Tuck, smiling, well accustomed to jokes about his name.

'So what news do you bring?'

'The abbot is aware of the murder investigation and is happy that you should use St Alban's as your incident room or murder room, whatever you want to call it.'

'That's what I wanted to hear. More teams are on their way so now I can assemble them and their equipment.' He dragged a mobile phone from his pocket and prodded a few buttons with his thick forefinger. Then he spoke into it. 'Brian, we've got the go-ahead for the premises we used last time at Maddleskirk Abbey, St Alban's Lecture Theatre. Make sure our teams find their way there. Some will be fetching equipment, computers, desks and so on.'

'Right, we'll cope,' said Inspector Lindsey, and all could hear his amplified responses.

'I'll address them as soon as they're all here. I don't want them hanging around doing nothing. By then we should know more than we do now. Got all that?'

'Yes, sir.'

Then he shoved his phone back into his pocket and addressed the monkstables. 'That was Detective Inspector Brian Lindsey who will be in charge of the murder room. Most of you have already met him. Right, Friar Tuck, it's time for me to address your merry men. Has everyone got a coffee? If not, organize a refill. Sit down, all of you. Make the place look tidy. And listen carefully.'

As everyone took their seats, the big man paddled around the room, reminding some observers of a seal trying to walk, then he stood at one end of the table and said, 'Right, ears pinned back! Not for the first time, I want to make use of your special skills and knowledge and that means you are part of my murder team. You might know that police forces are now making wider use of private security organizations, even in murder enquiries and other major crime investigations. You are all sworn constables; you are police officers so never forget that.

'Now, up in that woodland not far from the wishing well or holy pond or whatever you might call it, is a dead man. At this point we don't know who he is, where he is from, how he died or when he died. We'll know more when the post-mortem is complete. That is underway as I speak. Also underway is a forensic examination of the scene. We've no idea what we might discover near where the body was found or in the wider woodland. A weapon, hopefully. If it's hidden, we'll find it even if it's in the holy pond. And we might find something that will tell us chummy's name, where he's from and how he got there. Did he fall or was he pushed? There's a cliff overlooking the crime scene. Lots of questions to answer.'

He paused to allow his words to sink in, then continued, 'Identifying the victim is vital and that's where you come in. Ask around the college, the abbey and even the neighbouring villages to see whether a local man is missing – I'll issue a more detailed description eventually but we can get started now. He is about thirty years old, white skin, six feet tall or thereabouts with black hair and an athletic build. Dressed in a dark green T-shirt and blue jeans. That might be enough to be going on with but remember he could be a member of staff, a relation of someone working or living nearby. Someone from that construction site in the grounds. Or someone with absolutely no connection with the abbey, college or surrounding villages. A tourist perhaps? But whoever he is, or wherever he's from, someone must have seen him. We – you, that is – have to find that someone to see what he or she can tell us.'

He paused again for them to absorb his words, then resumed. 'Ask whether anyone saw him in the last couple of days or so. In these large grounds? Elsewhere? Alone or with someone? I don't think his body was carried up there. That would be almost impossible even for a team of two or three. I think he was killed nearby and his body dumped or thrown off that cliff with all identifying evidence removed.'

After another pause, he continued, 'Based on my experience plus some recent criminal intelligence, we're talking of professional villains, gentlemen. Gang warfare. Drugs related, more than likely. All the signs are there. I'm aware that such crimes are out of your league but you ought to be aware of them to understand what we're up against. In this case, a ritual-style stabbing is not out of the question. I am aware there have been several undetected murders elsewhere in Britain but this kind of stabbing was used in some of them. It's a sort of trademark but the killers have never been brought to justice even if some of us know who they are. Knowing who they are but finding the necessary evidence to support our belief is not always possible. Wounds can be made with all sorts of weapons but this is deep and narrow – think of a stiletto. That's a dagger with a long tapering blade, once highly fashionable. You can still buy Italian ones on the internet, some concealing their blades like flick-knives. Some call them switchblades. Or it could be a bayonet. So, gentlemen, this is what I want.

High priority! I want the victim named. I want the weapon traced. I want to know who has been tramping or visiting those woods in recent days. Why were they there? I want to know if you were aware of anyone arguing or being violent to each other. I want to know who enters that wood or climbs up to the wishing well regularly – dog walking perhaps, bird watching, just exploring. I want names of anyone who might have noticed something out of the ordinary. And I must be made aware of any illegal use of drugs hereabouts – even among pupils and staff. My detectives are assembling and will be briefed to under-take specific actions but as you are here now, we can begin our part of the investigation. Shall we meet back here at 1.30, after lunch? I know lunch is a fixed feast for you monks and I don't want to disrupt your routine more than necessary.'

He paused for a few seconds, then con-cluded, 'Friar Tuck will allocate your actions. Any questions?'

No one spoke.

'It all sounds fine to me, quite within our range of commitments,' said Prior Tuck.

'Good. Then get among the people right now. Find out who was staying here over the weekend. Be guided by Friar Tuck and meanwhile the county police and other forces will be told to search their records for a missing person who answers the description of our victim. That will be a nationwide check, by the way, thanks to computers. He could be someone who has wandered in here looking for the rest and refreshment for which the Benedictines are renowned. And don't overlook the drugs angle. Right, I'll see you all later. If you want me, I'll probably be in the St Alban's Lecture Theatre, otherwise Inspector Lindsey will know where to find me.'

As Napier was preparing to leave the room, one of the monks hailed him.

'Mr Napier, before you go, there is something else you should know.'

'And you are?'

'Father Will Stutely. There are two Father Wills here, the other is staffing the cop shop. Shall I tell him or will you, Father Prior?'

'You go ahead,' agreed Prior Tuck.

'Fire away,' invited Napier.

'One of our monks is missing.'

'Missing?'

'Since Saturday. He asked the other Father Will to hear confessions...'

'You mean folks still come and confess voluntarily?'

'Indeed they do!'

'Well, blow me! In my profession we have to drag confessions out of villains whilst hindered by rules and regulations ... mind, I don't think you'll get many folks confessing to murders and such! Sorry to interrupt.

Tell me about this monk.'

Father Will told his story, culminating with, 'Father Prior has persuaded the hospital – Scarborough Beach Hospital – to carry out a physical search of the premises, but according to hospital records, he never arrived and was not registered as a patient.'

'But you say he went to Scarborough Beach Hospital on Saturday evening? And got a lift there?'

'Yes, he was delivered at the hospital by one of our official drivers who then returned to the abbey.'

'And since then no word from him, or about him?'

'Nothing.'

'This is most odd and very intriguing,' grunted Napier. 'A monk goes missing shortly before a body is found in local woods. Ask yourselves this, reverend gentlemen – has he done a runner? Is he responsible for that death? Is that why he has fled the scene? Does he know something we should know? The coincidence and timing fit our story, don't they? In my job dealing with criminals, the whole thing stinks! And the location fits. In short, we need to find that monk – and quickly!'

No one responded.

'Well,' said Napier. 'The first thing I would say is we must carry out our own physical search of that hospital! It's no good relying on the staff, they've other things to do and they'll never do a proper search anyway. It's our duty because we have to regard the missing monk as a murder suspect. That means finding him and quizzing him closely. I'll get two Scarborough detectives to search the hospital immediately.'

'Let's hope we find him,' sighed Father Will.

'If we can't, nobody can. So tell me his name. And have we got a decent description?'

'He's Father John Attwood,' Prior Tuck told him.

'John Attwood?' Napier frowned. 'That name rings a bell somewhere in the deep recesses of my mind. For some reason drug dealing come to the surface of my thinking. Can someone tell me about this man? Is John Attwood his real name or his monk's alias?'

'His real name but here he is known as Father John,' confirmed Prior Tuck. 'He joined the monastery rather late in life. He's a widower, a mature man of about sixty-five, nearly six feet tall, grey hair thinning a little on top, well built, a very nice person. He's a retired builder. When he left here, he would be wearing a dark grey clerical suit and dog collar, not a monk's habit.'

'Easy enough to spot in a hospital then? Unless he's wearing hospital pyjamas. Right, leave this with me. We've got a lot going on already so pending any changes I'll see you all this afternoon and will update you then. If you learn anything new, let me know. I'll get my teams to carry out an investigation into his past which could be relevant. So, Friar Tuck, can I leave the organization of the local searches to you?'

'Of course. We've done it before!'

'Then we all know what we're doing. Right, let's get started.'

Chapter 4

As the monkstables began their tasks, Nick was directed to the Maddleskirk Abbey Retreat Centre (MARC), more popularly known as The Grange. It had once been a large country house of that name but upon the death of its last owner it had been purchased by the abbey trustees. It was ideal as an accommodation centre for people on retreat. It was rather like a small hotel with all the necessary facilities and was always busy with visitors.

The lady in charge was Mrs Ruth Morley, a very capable woman in her mid forties. Tall, dark haired and dressed in her smart blue and white uniform, she acted as receptionist, secretary and general overseer, and it was widely acknowledged that all areas of The Grange were clean, comfortable, efficient and welcoming – and the food was good! Its cheerful and efficient atmosphere was due undoubtedly to the dedication and capabilities of Mrs Morley. When Nick arrived she was working in her office, which adjoined the reception area. She rose with a smile as he approached the counter.

'Ah, Nick.' They had known one another for several years. 'How can I help?'

She was aware of his part-time role with the monkstables and was always very keen to help him with his special responsibilities.

'A man has been found dead in those woods just across the valley,' he explained. 'He was off the beaten track high among the trees at the foot of a cliff, not far from the old holy well. It wasn't an accidental death, Ruth, he had a wound that suggests murder. Some CID are already there. The murder room is based in St Alban's Lecture Theatre and I'm helping the monkstables who are trying to establish his identity and movements.'

'Oh my goodness! Not another murder here...'

'We've no plans to make this the murder capital of Yorkshire!' he responded. 'But the death is being investigated and the police are trying to identify the victim. I'm wondering whether he might have been staying here on retreat?'

'Which one? We've had two retreats recently. One was during last week and it finished on Friday afternoon. The other was during the weekend, assembling Saturday morning with people staying overnight till Sunday and dispersing at five o'clock.'

'It's possible the victim was one of your residents. Without his name, all we have to go on is a description. Will that help?'

'You can always try!'

'He's a young white man about thirty with dark hair, casually dressed in a dark green T-shirt and blue jeans. He's about six feet tall – that's all we know at the moment, we've no photos. That could describe thousands of young men. The problem is that he had nothing in his pockets that would help to identification of him. No wallet or rucksack, nothing. He wasn't even wearing a watch.'

'Well, I can tell you straightaway he wasn't on the weekend retreat. They were all women of varying ages – sixteen up to sixty, I'd guess, but we don't keep details of our guests' ages! I'll get the file for last week's arrivals – we had a dozen, male and female, with quite a lot of young people among them.'

'That sounds promising.'

'Give me a second. Come into my office. There's a chair.'

She lifted some papers from a cabinet and then found the relevant file on her computer.

'We combine the old and new,' she explained. 'Some guests don't have computers so we use snail mail but most of the young ones now book online.'

'Computers are taking over the world!' Nick joked.

'Well, so long as it's for the better. Right, I'll do a computer printout for you. The CID will need it, won't they? To check names?'

'They'll want details of everyone who has stayed here recently,' he agreed. 'It'll mean a physical check to see if they all got safely home. Obviously, those who were on these premises during last weekend are of special interest – they'll need to be eliminated from the inquiry. And of course, they might have noticed our man whilst they were here. CID will need to talk to them all.'

When he ran through the list of names she could not confirm that any of the young men fitted the description of the murder victim. She recalled one with ginger hair, one who was prematurely bald and a third who was very much overweight.

'So are these people on the premises the whole time?'

'Oh no, we take them to visit various locations, using abbey mini-coaches. As you know, we're surrounded with lots of ruined abbeys, all with a long Catholic history that is largely ignored or overlooked, and there are also modern convents and abbeys like ours. The Marian shrine at Osmotherley is always popular as is Egton Bridge through its association with the martyr, Nicholas Postgate, with Ampleforth Abbey always on our list of places to visit with its fine tea-room and shop.'

'You'll be rivalling the Holy Land next!'

'Well, it's true that all those places provide a great deal of spiritual interest to people who join our retreats. Sometimes we take them to the seaside at Sandsend, Whitby or Scarborough where they can walk along the beach with a monk to contemplate upon what they have been told. Those beach pilgrimages work very well and we also take some up to our moorland with its own religious history. We try hard to give them a varied perspective on their ancient faith and its long, turbulent and troubled history in this country.'

'It's a blessing someone does that! If you can provide a printout of these names, I'll give them to Detective Inspector Lindsey for his teams to work on. Thanks for your time, Ruth.'

'Always pleased to help, Nick. You'll keep me informed?'

'Of course, and if you recollect anything that could be relevant, let me know.'

When Nick entered the murder room, detectives were arriving from those police stations nearest Maddleskirk Abbey. Detective Inspector Lindsey was dividing them into teams of two, allowing a mix of men and women, each comprising a detective sergeant and a detective constable. He was allocating 'actions' to those who had arrived. An action was a specific task which they should investigate and then record the results in the ever-expanding computer files of the murder room.

Periodic conferences would ensure that the entire assembly knew the outcome of all the actions. Simple devices such as blackboards and whiteboards displayed the essential data: 'Victim – white male about thirty years old, dark hair, six feet one inch tall, dressed in dark green T-shirt and blue jeans. Identity not known. Believed to have been killed before his body was dumped.'

There was an additional note that said: 'NB. Cause of death may be a head injury to rear of skull – PM confirmation awaited. Weapon could be a firearm but more probably a stab weapon – *not found at scene*. It must be traced and preserved for forensic examination. *There could be a drugs or gangland link.* Location of body: near base of cliff in woodland to the east of the footpath leading through Ashwell Priory woods to the wishing well on the hilltop. This former holy well is now a pond on the hilltop and it is currently off limits to all except SOCO.'

The whiteboards and blackboards could be easily amended as the situation developed and they provided a simple but vital *aide memoire* for the teams.

There would be a full briefing once everyone had arrived.

'Got something for us?' asked Brian Lindsey as Nick entered.

'Not a lot,' he admitted, handing over the list of names. 'These people were on retreat at The Grange last week and this weekend but Mrs Morley doesn't recognize the victim as one of them.'

'We'll check all the names, thanks. If the victim isn't on these lists, his killer might be! Or these people could have seen something suspicious going on. We'll interview them all. So what are your plans?'

'I was wondering about those construction workers on the building site? Some have been here for months and look like being here for a long time. So could the victim – or the murderer – be one of them?'

'We've got them in mind, Nick. I've despatched two teams to the site to commence enquiries. The problem with large construction companies is that workers come and go at a bewildering rate, often unknown to anyone except a secretary in one of the site offices. Worse still, some are itinerant workers looking for jobs that pay cash, staying only for a day or two then moving on before the authorities find them. And some use false names! But we're on to it. If one of the men has gone missing, we'll find out but it's amazing how many John Browns, Bill Smiths, Teddy Bears and Mickey Mouses work on such projects! Anyway, we should know the result of the PM soon, that's bound to help us.'

'So where are the monkstables? Do you know?' Nick asked.

'Checking staff and students in buildings around the campus, asking if they've seen the victim. That'll take some time. They're asking if any member of staff hasn't turned up for work or whether anyone has noticed unusual activities here, particularly as they might involve drugs. After all, there are a lot of students here.'

'I'll go back to the Postgate Room, Brian. I'm sure there's something I could be doing.'

'If you're out of a job, we could always use your skills as a statement reader, Nick. You know what's required?'

'I do. I worked in several murder rooms when I was in the job.'

'Well, don't be afraid to join us. We know you well enough to co-opt you on to the inquiry. There's always work waiting in here. But go to your own conference room to see how things are going, and keep in touch.'

The statement readers' work was vital to the success of a murder investigation. As the teams questioned potential witnesses, all their statements were written down and then processed by computer in the murder room. This meant that names, timing, vehicles and other salient details were abstracted and recorded in a master file on a dedicated computer. This enabled detailed cross-checks to be made and possible links established, thus providing fuel for further enquiries.

Nick decided to call at the cop shop to update Father Will on what Napier had revealed. He would also check whether Father Will had received any more news or information. Then he would go to the Postgate Room to await the eventual return of the monkstables. If there was no one around and nothing to do, he might go home. DI Lindsey's offer to employ him as a statement reader was very pleasing but, in view of the lapse of time since leaving the force, he felt that modern detectives with up-to-date equipment would be far more useful. They knew how to abstract every possible piece of evidence from statements and how to develop enquiries from what had been revealed. They had a deep understanding and professional knowledge of the police computer network, mobile phones, ATMs, credit cards and other sophisticated methods that could help in tracing a person's movements and whereabouts.

When he arrived at the cop shop, Father Will was working on the computer and had left the door standing open as a means of encouraging people to enter.

'Ah, Nick.' He smiled. 'Any developments?'

'Nothing dramatic. The murder teams are assembling and already the first are busy with enquiries. The monkstables are out and about the campus, trying to get a name or sighting of the victim whilst also checking for staff absentees. We've not heard from the pathologist so we don't know the official cause of death.'

'Was he stabbed?' As he asked the question, Father Will suddenly blushed and covered his mouth with his hand. He looked very flustered. 'Sorry, I shouldn't have asked that! Forget I asked, Nick. Please.'

'We haven't had confirmation from the post-mortem yet but Mr Napier believes it could be a stab wound at the base of the skull. It's a trademark of some gang executions linked to drugs. Can I ask why you asked that question?'

'It was nothing, I was being silly...' But his demeanour and the embarrassment on his face told Nick something was wrong and that it was troubling him deeply. 'Forget I asked that, Nick. Please. You must forget I asked that question. It's of no consequence.'

Father Will seemed to be getting himself deeper and deeper into some kind of mental turmoil and Nick felt he should offer help, especially if it was connected to his monk-stable work.

'If it's bothering you, you can tell me in confidence,' Nick offered. 'If it's connected to this murder, we need to know, whatever it is.'

'I can't say any more, I've said too much already,' the monk insisted, still looking highly agitated. 'Look, Nick, please ignore what I've just said. I must have overheard someone talking about a stabbing. People are talking, you know, about the murder. Word has got around already so I must learn to keep my mouth shut and not repeat gossip.'

'We can all be guilty of that!' Nick tried to make light of whatever was worrying Father Will but he could see it was causing deep concern. He tried to look him in the eyes but Will did not meet his gaze, turning his eyes away and licking his lips like a child trying to conceal some misdemeanour.

'Sorry, Nick,' was all he said.

'All right. I'll say no more, Father Will. But you know I'm always here if you need to talk. I mean that. In confidence, of course. There are times police officers are rather like confessors—'

'Thank you.' The monk cut off the end of Nick's sentence.

With some reluctance, Nick left the cop shop, leaving Father Will alone with his worries. He walked slowly through the deserted corridors of the mighty abbey church towards the Postgate Room, wondering whether Father Will knew the murder victim had died by stabbing. If so, how could he know that? And would it be connected with Father John's disappearance? Was there some kind of mischief going on within this monastic place of peace?

In the background were sounds of the monks' choir rehearsing Psalm IV which they would later sing at Compline; the huge abbey church was filled with their singing and organ music. On the surface, everything seemed at peace – but that was far from the case. A man had been murdered very close to the abbey and one of the monkstables appeared to be deeply troubled while another monk had disappeared. Nick walked into the deserted Postgate Room and made himself a cup of coffee as the sound of monks' distant singing created an air of unreality.

Then the door opened and in walked Father Alban. He had been visiting some college buildings to ask about missing men. He had returned to update the records and helped himself to a cup of coffee, chattering as he made the drink.

'I've finished in the accommodation blocks and buildings around St Peter's House. I've talked to housemasters, teachers, cleaners and students, but to their knowledge no one's missing. And all denied there was a drug problem on site.'

'No luck with his identification then?' Nick asked.

'Nothing. No one can help with identifying him. I asked them to cast their minds back to Friday or Saturday but the answer was the same. Nothing. They've seen nothing unusual and know nothing.'

'Well, you can update the records so we are all aware of that, then what are you doing next?'

'I thought I would conduct a similar exercise at the sports centre just behind St Peter's. I couldn't remember whether or not I was allocated it earlier. If someone's already been, I can find somewhere else to ask my questions. But I'm dying for a coffee – I'm parched! I'm not accustomed to talking so much and asking all these questions!'

'Well, take the weight off your feet for a few minutes and enjoy the coffee. While we're alone, I must say I'm rather worried about Father Will Redman. He's doing a stint in the cop shop now. It was something he said to me not many minutes ago that caused my concern.'

'Will it help to tell me?'

'Yes, it will. I was telling him about the murder victim and he asked if he'd been stabbed. The minute the words were out of his mouth, he became all embarrassed and worried and said he shouldn't have mentioned that. I asked why he'd mentioned stabbing but he wouldn't tell me; he wouldn't say another word about it and asked me to forget he'd ever spoken that word. I don't want to pry and I don't want to cause him unnecessary upset but it is all very odd. I must say it has bothered me. Now can I ask you not to repeat this to him?'

'Of course. The only thing I can think is that he had to stand in at confessions on Saturday night for Father John Attwood, who had a medical appointment. I saw Will afterwards and I could see he was far from happy even then. Something was troubling him deeply and I wondered if it was something he'd heard under the seal of confession. If so, he can never talk about it. Not to anyone, not even to his abbot. Not ever. If it is a burden he heard in confession, he must bear that burden alone. That's how things are. It's one of the difficulties of being a priest. All I can say is that he needs our prayers.'

'Are you saying that if someone confessed to stabbing another person, even to the point of killing them, the priest couldn't inform the police?'

'That's exactly what I'm saying, Nick. The seal of confession is absolute.'

'It makes me wonder how many murderers have convinced priests of their future good conduct merely to gain absolution!'

'We will never know. But if it is possible that Father Will did hear something along those lines during a confession, I must ask you not to press him about it.'

'I understand. So what should I do?'

'Nothing, Nick. Absolutely nothing. And don't mention it again, especially not to Father Will or the police. It is best forgotten entirely because there is nothing you or anyone else can do. It's over. Finished.'

'So if the post-mortem reveals that our murder victim died from a stab wound, I cannot ask Father Will to reveal the identity of the person who confessed? I don't know how to respond to that.'

'Say nothing and do nothing, Nick. Don't worry about Father Will – he's part of our community and we'll care for him. He'll not be the first priest to undergo such soul-searching, and he'll not be the last. Now I must go.'

Nick tried to settle down to some updating of his clerical work but found it difficult to concentrate. Then the phone rang. It was Detective Inspector Lindsey.

'Ah, Nick, glad I caught you. We've got the result of the postmortem. First things first. A detailed search of the victim's clothing and body confirm that he had no form of identification upon him. No wallet, credit cards, driving licence, tattoos, operation scars, nothing. Nothing left at the scene either but one thing was overlooked by his killer. His jeans have a designer label whose origins we'll trace. We've still no idea who he is, but we are re-checking his fingerprints and DNA as well as circulating a description through police networks.'

'And the cause of death? Has that been determined?'

'Yes, it has. He had a neck wound but he also had bone breakages that were consistent with him falling from a height after death – thrown down perhaps, or perhaps he fell. However, he was stabbed at the back of his head, close to where the skull absorbs the spinal column. It's called the cerebellum. A slim long-bladed dagger, a stiletto, was probably used. It damaged the vertebrae and severed the blood vessels in his neck. He would have died almost instantly. It's a trademark execution by some drugs cartels – and it's not restricted to other drug dealers. Anyone who angers them might get the treatment. We believe many of their murders remain undiscovered because they dispose of the body and other evidence.'

Lindsey paused to allow Nick to write a summary on a scrap of paper before he asked, 'So a simple stiletto dagger could cause that kind of serious wound?'

'It could. A bayonet can't be ruled out.

And the killer would be very strong. And determined. He's sliced the main blood vessels in the throat and neck, the carotids. The weapon has not been found so further searches will be undertaken.'

'You'll be arranging those?' asked Nick.

'Leave it to me. If the weapon is not found, the killer may still have it in his or her possession and it will bear traces of the victim's blood even if an attempt's been made to clean it. The fact the killer still has the weapon makes him or her very dangerous, and it might have been used for previous killings although many killers like to get rid of the murder weapon. Will you warn your monkstables to be constantly alert, especially when they are interviewing people?'

'I will.' Nick felt sure the man's injuries could be described as a stabbing. 'Just one other thing, Brian. This appears to be the work of a major criminal so do we still believe it's a gangland killing?'

'We might have to revise that thinking, Nick. It could be a copy-cat killing. We have an open mind at the moment.'

'But we think the victim was dead before he hit the ground?'

'Almost certainly. We have a SOCO team examining the ground at the top of that cliff; they might find blood up there. The stab wound would have been enough to kill him.'

'So his "fall" was really a means of disposing of the body?' suggested Nick, thinking of Father Will in that confessional.

'Yes, it was. If it hadn't been for Barnaby, his remains might never have been found.'

Chapter 5

Alone in the Postgate Room, Nick found himself deeply troubled by the unexplained absence of Father John and could not prevent his thoughts returning to Father Will. Whatever had happened after he'd swapped duties with Father John was obviously preying on his conscience – so Nick decided to visit the confessional, not to confess any sins but to examine it. He would try to visualize it as it would have been on Saturday night. Could those penitents be traced? If so, could they have noticed anything out of the ordinary that evening?

Could one of them have confessed to Father Will that he or she had stabbed a man? Or worse, had someone confessed to *murder?* A stabbing was not necessarily murder; it included wounding, even slightly. But was it feasible that Father Will could have heard a confession of murder? If he had, was the penitent one of those who had queued on Saturday night from six o'clock until seven?

That was around the time Father John would be at Scarborough Beach Hospital awaiting the result of his blood analysis or cancer readings. It was an awful thought, but could Father John have killed the man before vanishing on a fictitious trip?

The question was whether the victim was alive on Saturday, the day the confessions were heard? He had not been *found* dead until Monday morning – this morning – but his time of death had not been determined. Is that what was troubling Father Will? A penitent confessing to murder by stabbing? And then seeking absolution?

Nick had heard that this was the most difficult of confessions a priest might ever hear. During their training for the priesthood, they were taught the necessary response and advice they should give but nonetheless all dreaded having to listen as someone actually confessed to murder, particularly one that remained unsolved. A killer confessing to murder once he or she had been convicted created less of a problem for a priest.

As Nick headed for the south transept where the confessional was located he was considering ways of identifying the people who had been there on Saturday night. If a small gathering had assembled between 6 p.m. and 7 p.m., either to queue to go to confession or simply to sit quietly in prayer, then each would have been aware of the others. The chances were that most were local people known to one another, or to the staff or brethren of the abbey. Already, it seemed Nick's task was feasible. If a stranger had been noticed among them, he or she was likely to be regarded as a suspect.

The route from the Postgate Room into the abbey church led through long wide corridors of highly polished marble, many with drawings, photographs or paintings along their walls. They depicted the history and development of the abbey.

This was a modern abbey built in the early 1960s although it had been constructed over the ruins of an earlier priory that now formed the crypt and undercroft beneath the present church. Although it was a Catholic abbey, it lacked much of the splendour and highly coloured decor of its contemporaries, especially those overseas, although it exuded a strong spiritual atmosphere that suggested silence and respect.

In that silence, and with due respect, Nick made his way along the deserted corridors into the south transept, genuflecting before the high altar as sacred organ music filled the church.

The confessional, duly soundproofed, was built into a corner of that transept. Alone in this quiet place, he moved into a pew that provided a view of the complete transept and knelt down to make it appear he was in private prayer. He tried to imagine this area busy with people, as indeed it had been on Saturday night. They had been sitting or kneeling here, possibly with a murderer amongst them.

As he looked around, Nick noticed the name-board above the door of the confessional; it continued to bear the name of Father John Attwood as the confessor. Although he was a recent addition to the monks of this abbey, he was not a monkstable. Nick's eyes ranged around this place through which he had regularly passed without having had any reason to pause and reflect. Now he noticed various interesting gadgets on the walls and suspended from the ceiling. A fire alarm, a loud speaker linked to the lectern on the high altar, a system for lowering the lights for replacement bulbs and repairs – and several security cameras. They were now essential in churches due to thefts of valuables ranging from silver candlesticks to furnishings via statues and offertory boxes. They were also installed on the exterior, to deter thieves, especially those who stole lead from the roofs.

Would those cameras have been activated on Saturday night? If so, would they have captured the images of those people awaiting their turn for confession? There was absolutely no way cameras or listening devices would be installed *inside* the confessionals. He wondered whose job it was to monitor the footage?

If the cameras had been operating would the images be sufficiently clear for a viewer to identify faces? But whatever their capabilities, the cameras offered hope. But was such an enquiry within Nick's area of responsibility or should he suggest it to Prior Tuck or a monkstable? Or to Napier's team?

As he continued to kneel, he decided he must not initiate these enquiries. It would be an abuse of trust in this hallowed place; he was fully aware of the sanctity of the confessional. On the other hand as a former police officer and now security adviser to the abbey, he could not ignore the fact that valuable images may be present in the security system. They may be highly important in establishing creditable witnesses to recent events – and could unmask a killer.

The answer was to inform Detective Chief Superintendent Napier. This piece of information must be considered part of the murder investigation. It was not a task for the monkstables even though it might help to trace Father John. Nick left his pew, genuflected and made his way out of the south door and down the steps onto the road that would take him to St Alban's Lecture Theatre. Three minutes later he was entering the murder room, which was now noisy and busy as more detectives had arrived and were being briefed by DI Lindsey.

During a lull, he noticed Nick and called, 'Anything I can do, Nick?'

'I'd like a word with Mr Napier if that's possible.'

'Just knock on his door, the green one. That's what he tells us to do.'

'Thanks.'

He did so and a voice called, 'Don't hang about out there, come in, I won't bite,' and so he walked in. Napier had managed to squeeze his desk and a computer into a tiny ante room that was full of stored easels, blackboards and other lecturing necessities.

'So what brings you here, Nick? Sit down if you can find a seat.'

He found a stool and began. 'You might think what I'm going to say now is off limits, Mr Napier, but maybe you're not familiar with churches, religion, monks and so forth?'

'I'm not a God botherer, Nick, but doing my job among the great English public has taught me a little about the Catholic faith. Even so, I'm still puzzled that folks come to your church and voluntarily confess to all manner of things to a priest. I wish my job was so simple! I need to know something about everything otherwise I'd get no detecting done! So don't hold back, tell me what's troubling you.'

'It centres upon the sacrament of confession,' he began.

'I was taught about that on my CID training course, Nick. I know that if chummy confesses something to a Catholic priest, the priest can never reveal it to anyone, never. But that is not English law, Nick. Our laws recognize that the priest is governed by his Church and in practice we and our legal friends would not demand that a priest broke the seal of confession. But in law, the priest cannot claim that legal privilege as a right – but it is a privilege that's widely accepted. It is, and always will be, a difficult area within our laws of evidence. How's that? See, I remembered my lectures from training school days.'

'I'm impressed!'

'So what's all this got to do with what you want to tell me?'

Nick explained his concerns about Father Will, relating the words he had used and trying to replicate his physical appearance of shock. 'It was his reference to stabbing, Mr Napier. When I mentioned the body in the woods, he asked if the victim had been stabbed, then immediately withdrew his comments. It made me wonder if he knew something about it. It was one of the other monks who wondered if Will had heard a worrying sort of confession. Priests must be affected by what they hear...'

'Aye, lad, they must but if we try to extract that information, they will not reveal it. It's happened before with other crimes, Nick, and there's nothing we can do. I know. I've tried. Were you going to suggest something?'

He explained about the security cameras in the south transept, and how that particular session of confession had occurred between 6 p.m. and 7 p.m. on Saturday, with Father Will standing in at short notice when Father Attwood had been called away to hospital.

'There could be something there for us. Do you think my teams might turn up something useful from the cameras?'

'I thought if we searched the images that show people queuing for confession on Saturday evening, we might find our killer among them. I know it's a shot in the dark and I have no firm evidence of what the priest heard from the killer, but if we can identify him, it would be a good beginning.'

'Him? Why do you think it's a man?'

'I just thought–'

'Never pre-judge, Nick. Killers can be male or female. If we search that security film, we'll be looking for a man or a woman. Although our victim was stabbed, deeply stabbed – would a woman have the strength to do that? And extract the dagger afterwards? Sometimes knives cannot be hauled out of stab wounds due to the suction.'

'I thought his neck had been cut—'

'Cut, yes, and stabbed down to the vertebrae. I've seen it on the computer screen direct from the slab in the morgue. A deep thrust, Nick. Entry at the back of the neck. With a very sharp and short tapering blade. Like a stiletto. Stilettos are still around, Nick, even if they are out of fashion. So if – and I stress *if* – your monk heard someone confess to a stabbing, whatever the weapon used, it is of interest to us.'

'There's no way of knowing whether he heard a confession to murder, Mr Napier.'

'There isn't but this is a very interesting development, Nick, and something I might have overlooked, so thank you. Neither you nor I want to lose favour with the brethren in this place so leave this to me. I'll keep you out of it. I'll obtain that security film as part of our overall inquiry and when it comes to searching, I'll get one of the monkstables to identify those who were queuing for confession. I suspect most will be regulars, local people known to the priests, but it will be a good start. I accept there may have been strangers among them. I hope we can trace them and have words. Who knows, we might also obtain a confession to a stabbing! How does that sound?'

'You've put my mind at rest, thanks.'

'This could be the breakthrough we need. I appreciate your efforts, Nick. Now show me that confessional box? If it's going to be an integral part of our enquiries, I need to have a look at it.'

During the short walk, Nick asked Napier, 'Have we an identity for our victim?'

'Nothing, no. We're having his fingerprints checked as I speak; we got some good images from the body. DNA samples have been taken as well but DNA analysis takes longer. If he hasn't any convictions, his fingerprints won't be much help. Failing that, we've now got details of who made his shoes, jeans and T-shirt, so we might be able to trace them to a local retailer who can remember him buying them. If he used a credit card, we can trace him. In other words, there's a long way to go, always slow and time-consuming. But we usually get there. And a motive? At this stage I haven't a clue except we might have got ourselves into something big so we must put a name to him. Now, have your monk-stables discovered anything I should know about?'

'Only the stabbing question. They've not had reports of anyone missing from their places of work or their usual haunts – apart from Father John – and we've no leads on identification of the victim, no sightings in this area. Ah, here we are, this is the entrance to the south transept.'

Nick led him up the steps and into the transept. A monk was in the organ loft practising and the entire abbey church was filled with his sacred music, the composer of which was unknown to Nick but he thought it was the music of one of the Gregorian chants.

'Nice,' whispered Napier. 'Music like that always pleases me.'

'This is the confessional.' Nick showed him the door in the wall on the north side; it was a solid oak door with small opaque glass panels near the top to permit entry of a modicum of light. Beside it was an identical panel which was not a door and on the wall nearby was a name-board still showing 'Father John Attwood'.

'So where are the cameras?'

Nick pointed to sites on the ceiling and around the walls, adding that some of the equipment consisted of loud speakers linked to the lectern and even the organ loft.

'So who looks after the cameras, Nick? Any idea?'

'Sorry, no. The prior will tell you.'

'I don't want to involve you in this, Nick. We might be talking delicate and confidential stuff here. So how does this confessional function?'

Nick explained how the penitents awaited their turns in the pews of the south transept and when the previous person emerged from the confessional box, the next entered via the door that faced the pews. He explained that the interior comprised of two soundproofed cubicles, one used by the priest who entered via a door to the rear, out of sight from the transept, with the other being used by the penitent.

'So he sits there out of sight but in verbal contact as folks confess all their sins to him, is that how it works?'

'Basically that's it.'

'It's a rum do if you ask me and I bet he gets some wonderful stories. Do you get thieves confessing to shoplifting, rioters admitting criminal damage and sex offenders explaining why they do such things?'

'I don't know, but I guess the whole world of nastiness is confessed in there, Mr Napier.'

'Even murders?'

'Even murders,' Nick agreed.

'Can you show me the interior of that cubicle? I've never examined one of these before today. Never had the need.'

As there was no one in the abbey church except the monk now playing the 'Miserere mei,' Nick led Napier to the door and opened it. As he did so, a small electric light illuminated the interior of the confessional, about the size of a public telephone kiosk. By holding the door open, they could see the kneeler in front of the far wall and the small grille above it, at head level for someone on their knees.

'A tight squeeze for a chap like me,' said

Napier, grinning. 'How often is it cleaned?'

'Once a week I guess,' was all Nick could answer. 'To be honest, I've no idea. Why do you ask?'

'I was thinking it's a good place to hide stolen goods ... you know, she nicks stuff from the school shop, hides it while she makes her confession, then leaves it to collect later. See, there's something under the kneeler, shining in the light.'

'Most folks would never think of looking in here for stolen property,' Nick began.

'I'm not most folks, Nick.' He stepped in to lift up the kneeler. There was a lot of dust beneath it but that didn't interest him as he stooped for a closer look. He placed the portable kneeler outside and then bent closer to examine an object that Nick could not see.

'You'll never guess what I've found here, Nick.'

'Sweet papers? Drinks bottles? Umbrella?'

'No, something much more interesting. A stiletto dagger.'

Chapter 6

'Don't touch it!' snapped Napier.

Nick was at a loss for words. He wondered where the stiletto had come from, how long it had been there and who had left it; all inane questions but all desperately important. But the most important – was it the murder weapon? – could only be answered by scientific examination. Had the man in the woods been killed with that stiletto and if so how had it come to be hidden beneath the kneeler in a confessional?

For several long silent moments Napier stood as still as a rock with his chin in one hand as he stared the stiletto, sometimes stooping down for a closer look at tiny objects he'd spotted among the dust, but not touching anything.

'This could be what we're looking for. This entire area must be cordoned off. The confessional is out of bounds from this moment, except to Scenes of Crime officers. It's a crime scene now. Guarding it is a task for your monkstables in uniform. I'll set things in motion right away. We need to wrap this place in yellow tape, lock the south door and prevent access until I say otherwise. We need to go through the dust and debris in the confessional, check every inch of it for possible fingerprints and DNA deposits, then examine the CCTV film especially where people are queuing to tell their priest how naughty they've been and how many murders they've committed.'

'Does it mean we have to close the entire abbey church?'

'I can't see that's necessary; this is the area that concerns us. Now, while I call the murder room to get things moving, you go and lock that south door. I see there's a mighty bar inside that will secure it, just like the good old days when church doors were strong enough to keep an army out.'

'No problem.'

'Then if you want to be helpful, can you call your cop shop and arrange for a couple of uniformed monkstables to come and stop inquisitive visitors entering this south transept from inside the church whilst it's a crime scene. You'll need to tell the abbot as well. I can't see him being very pleased that we're going to cordon off part of his church.'

'He'll understand,' was all Nick could think of saying.

While Napier was making his arrangements, Nick felt it would be a quick and simple matter to walk to the cop shop and recruit a couple of monkstables for security duties.

'I'm going to the cop shop to find a pair of monkstables,' he told Napier.

'Do that, then come straight back here, Nick. And don't tell anyone what we've found here, not yet. Leave that to me. The element of surprise can sometimes prove useful. I'll guard this place for the time being.'

As Nick left, he heard Napier's loud voice saying into his mobile phone, 'Napier here, Brian. I'm in the south transept of the abbey church. I've found something that could be evidence. We need to cordon off the transept, not the whole church, and we'll need SOCO here, and the photographer. A full crime scene examination is necessary. Your teams will need to use the north entrance to the church, I've locked the south door. I'll be waiting inside to explain things.'

'Understood, boss. I'll see to it now.'

Father Will was still staffing the counter of the cop shop and showed signs of nervous anxiety as Nick approached.

'Father Will, can you find a couple of uniformed monkstables for me? There should be some in the grounds on those earlier enquiries. Can you divert them from their current task and ask them to come immediately to the south transept but not via the south door, it's locked.'

'Yes, yes, of course, Nick. It's no problem.

Can I ask why they are required?'

'Detective Chief Superintendent Napier has found what might be evidence in the murder investigation. He wants to secure the entire scene.'

'That's where the confessional's located.'

'It is, Father, yes.'

'Can I ask what he has found?'

'We're not sure yet.' Nick told a white lie. 'It has to be forensically examined but it might not be linked to the murder.'

'Will he want to talk to me?'

'I'm sure he will in view of the fact you replaced Father John Attwood. He might want to know whether you noticed anything curious or anyone behaving strangely on Saturday evening. I should say that he hasn't told me this – this is my own reading of the circumstances.'

'Well, I'll help all I can, you know that, but equally you know I can't say everything...'

'Yes, I understand, but I think Mr Napier is finding that difficult.'

When Nick returned to the south transept a team of detectives had arrived and were placing yellow plastic ribbons across the entrance from the nave. They formed a very effective barrier and soon afterwards two uniformed monkstables – Fathers John Little and Mutch Miller – arrived. Their instructions were simple: they had to prevent any unauthorized person entering the crime scene.

Nick stood outside the tape barrier, hoping to catch Napier's eye as further Scenes of Crime officers arrived to be briefed. Eventually Napier spotted him and came across to speak.

'There's nothing for you here, Nick. It's all down to our scientific wizards but I do want a word.' He pointed to the name-plate beside the confessional. 'You told me that this monk had swapped with another on Saturday evening? Father Will?'

'That's right.'

'And we've still no word about the disappearance of Father John. I've still got officers searching the hospital in Scarborough but so far with no luck. But they're a good team, they're searching every niche and every likely hiding place even though the hospital authorities continue to deny he ever arrived.'

'We know he arrived; the official driver confirms that.'

'Yes, but did he actually go into the hospital? The hospital insists no member of staff telephoned to call him in. If that's true, who rang him? Someone did. And where from? And why? Or has he made up the whole story? That missing monk is exercising our minds, Nick – we can't overlook the fact he's in the frame for the murder. Can you go and have a word with the driver who delivered him? Just to make a double-check that he is absolutely sure Father John went into the hospital?'

'I'll do it now.'

'It goes without saying that I'll need to talk to Father Will. He might recollect someone placing something on the floor of the confessional. What happens to stuff that is left in there? Handbags, umbrellas, books or whatever?'

'They're taken to reception: there's a cabinet for found property so that losers can reclaim their belongings. Most of the stuff does get reclaimed.'

'But not a hidden stiletto, I suspect. Especially if it's a murder weapon. I'll have a word with those in reception to see if anyone's ever left other dangerous objects. I'd no idea these voluntary confessions could be so productive! It makes me think we should examine every confessional after every set of confessions... Who knows what we might turn up!'

'I'll bet there aren't many stilettos, Mr Napier!'

'One's enough to be going on with.'

And so Nick left him and went to have a chat with the driver. It was a five-minute walk across the grounds to the transport department, with its four drivers, two full-time mechanics and a variety of vehicles. He was looking for Tim Farley, an experienced driver in his mid-fifties who had previously run his own taxi business. He was outside the garages hosing down a Vauxhall.

'Now, Mr Rhea, what brings you here? Is it to do with Father John again?'

'You've been asked already?'

'Aye, one of the detectives, I told him what I knew. They're searching the hospital for him right now.'

'Do you mind if I repeat the questioning? I've been asked to do so by Detective Chief Superintendent Napier.'

'No, fire away. There's not a lot I can tell you.'

'Let's start with the basics, Tim. Father John Attwood asked you to take him to the Beach Hospital in Scarborough last Saturday evening. Is that true?'

'Yes, it is, and that's what I did. I picked him up outside the monastery at five o'clock and drove him to the hospital, getting him there just before the time of his appointment. It was about ten minutes to six when we got there.'

'Were you supposed to bring him back the same evening?'

'That was the original arrangement but he said he had no idea how long his appointment would be and he'd find his own way back here. Taxi, I expect, or mebbe a bus. So I just dropped him off at the main entrance and came back empty.'

'The main entrance?'

'Well, nearby. There was an empty parking space on the approach road so I pulled in to let him out. He thanked me and I drove off.'

'So where did he go? Did you notice?'

'I must admit I thought it odd because he didn't head for the main entrance and reception as you'd expect. It was still daylight and I saw a woman waiting for him. She was in the shadows under some trees so I didn't get a good look at her.'

'Can you give a brief description?'

'Very sketchy. Medium height, slim build, no hat, fair hair well dressed in a dark blue skirt and light blue jacket ... long sleeves...'

'Her age?'

'Dunno. You can never be certain with women's ages! Forty-five, mebbe. Even fifty. Somewhere about there at a guess.'

'That's not bad for just a glance! Do you think he knew her?'

'I can't be sure, Nick. I think not because I had my window down and heard her ask him, "Father Attwood?"'

'So she was expecting him?'

'So it seemed. I thought she was waiting for him. She'd have recognized him as a priest because he was wearing a grey suit and clerical collar. Not his monk's habit, not on a trip like that. But she checked it was the right person.'

'So what happened next?'

'I heard her say something like, "Your specialist unit is this way, Father," and she led him away from the main entrance.'

'On foot?'

'Yes, although she might have had a car parked nearby – but if so, I never saw it.'

'Did you see him again, or hear from him?'

'Nothing, no.'

'And what about the journey to Scarborough? Was he chatty with you? Explaining why he was going to hospital?'

'No, he wasn't, he was a bit on the quiet side although he said the trip was to do with his prostate cancer. They'd found something in a blood sample, so he said. But nothing else. He's usually very chatty and interesting when I take him anywhere and generally sits in the front passenger seat but this time he sat in the back and hardly said a word the whole trip.'

'What did you make of that?'

'I thought he must be bothered about his cancer, Nick. Worrying about this unexpected summons to see the specialist.'

'He said he'd been summoned, did he?'

'He said he'd got a phone call, right out of the blue and at short notice, so he got Father Will to swap duties with him. He wasn't sure what he was going to be told about his cancer. No one had given him any idea.'

'Has he been before? To that hospital? For his cancer treatment?'

'No, he told me he usually went to York. I don't know why he had to attend Scarborough this time. He never said; in fact, I don't think he knew either.'

'The hospital authorities swear they never made the call and that he was never admitted,' remarked Nick. 'They've checked. He never arrived.'

'Well, he said he had to go there, he had all the details on a piece of paper, he'd taken it all down from the phone call. And that woman was waiting for him. That means he hadn't made up the story.'

'I agree with you. You said you've been interviewed before about this?'

'Only briefly. One of those CID chaps came to ask me if I'd delivered Father Attwood to the Scarborough Beach Hospital and I told him I had. He never asked if I'd seen what happened to him – I just said I'd dropped him outside the main entrance where he was met by a woman from the specialist unit but explained I'd not brought Father John back here.'

'Someone might want to discuss this in greater depth, Tim. Detective Chief Superintendent Napier is showing an increased interest in our missing monk. Somewhat mysteriously, Father John seems to have disappeared into thin air.'

'That woman definitely led him off to a specialist unit, I heard her say so.'

'I'm told the hospital doesn't have any external specialist units, Tim. Everything's on the same site.'

'Mebbe it was a private clinic he was going to?'

'You could be right; we'll check on that. We have to ask whether this is a voluntary disappearance, or whether something has happened, like kidnapping. From what you noticed, it does seem he never entered the hospital and that he was never forced into anything. Now another question – do you know whether there are CCTV cameras at the hospital entrance?'

'I'm sure there are. Parking is restricted to twenty minutes and there are notices to say the vehicles are timed in and out by cameras.'

'Then they might have recorded Father John's arrival and liaison?'

'It's worth a check. Most hospitals have security cameras all over the place. Is this summat to do with that dead body in the woods?'

'That can't be ruled out, Tim. The fact these things have all happened virtually at the same time could be relevant – but we don't know yet. All I can say is that the police are looking into every possibility.'

'It looks like Father John knows summat!'

'We'll never know until we ask him. And for that, we must find him.'

'Well, if I can help more, just ask, Nick. And

in the meantime, I'll keep my ears and eyes open. Doing my job does let me overhear a lot of private chatter, just like a London taxi driver! Oh, and by the way, Father John didn't have a mobile phone with him. He reckons he doesn't need one, so he told me.'

Nick thanked Tim, who returned to his depot while Nick headed back to relay the gist of his conversation to CID. He went directly into the abbey church, thinking Napier might still be in the south transept but he wasn't. The stiletto would not be moved until SOCO had completed their examination of the scene. Some boffins were still working in and around the confessional box but Nick had no idea of the present whereabouts of the stiletto and did not stop to ask. Upon being told that Napier had returned to the murder room, he headed in that direction only to find that half the number of CID had been relieved for lunch. The others would go later. They were using one of the college dining rooms but Napier made it clear he could not accept free meals. The police must pay their dues.

Napier, already seated as Nick entered, noticed him. 'Nick, here, man, here. We need to talk and now is an ideal time. Where's Friar Tuck? Does he lunch with Robin Hood and his Merry Men? Get yourself a plateful and come and join me.'

'Prior Tuck might be in the monks'

refectory, being a monk.'

'Oh well, I'll have to make do with you, Nick. So how was your chat with that driver?'

As Napier demolished the contents of his plate and went back for a second helping, Nick outlined his chat with Tim Farley. The big man seldom interrupted – he was too busy eating – but grunted acknowledgements from time to time.

'Thanks for doing that, Nick,' he said eventually. 'This confirms our information about Attwood's visit to the hospital – in short, he never went inside. Our physical search confirms that and a check of the computer and other records shows he was never admitted as a patient. There is no record of him attending that hospital. There's no record of a telephone call to him either. His cancer file is kept at York – we've checked there and York didn't direct him to Scarborough. So either he made up the whole story about going for a consultation or someone persuaded him to visit Scarborough Beach Hospital on a realistic pretext. Both those suggestions raise the question – why? Can we link him with the murder? That's the big question. And who was that woman he met? We need to find her.'

'I think they were strangers to one another. She asked his name although there's no doubt she was expecting him. It means he might have been in Scarborough at the time of the victim's death,' suggested Nick. 'If so, surely that's an alibi?'

'It could be if we knew the precise time of his death, which we don't. I'll despatch a Scarborough CID officer to the hospital to search its CCTV films. What would we do without modern technology?'

'I daren't think about that!'

'Well, whatever the problems, we must find John. I would go so far as to suggest that is now high priority.'

'So you know something we don't?' suggested Nick.

'Yes, I do. The chief has discussed this case with me but there are things I can't reveal yet,' admitted Napier. 'I will tell you that our chat involved the man known as John Attwood but I can't reveal the reason at this stage. There's more work to do before the three o'clock conference. What I hope to say to you all then will be the *real* beginning of this operation!'

Nick noticed that Napier used the word *operation* instead of investigation. But he made no comment.

Chapter 7

Detective Chief Superintendent Napier had not yet revealed the change of direction in the inquiry. He had been ordered by his chief constable to develop it into a highly secret sting operation codenamed Rainbow. It would run conjointly with the murder investigation. The intention, after urgent discussions with the relevant agencies including SOCA (the Serious Organised Crime Agency), was to draw into a well-crafted web a criminal who was noted for murder, vicious cruelty, drug dealing and huge wealth. The plan was to capture him whilst securing sufficient evidence to convict him. He had a criminal record but was currently able to keep several steps ahead of any investigating team. Already Napier was being assisted by several secretive security agencies. Whether or not the whole truth could or should be revealed to every member of his murder team at this early stage was a decision he would soon have to make. Meanwhile, security was of paramount importance.

Similarly, the extent of information that could or should be passed to ex-Inspector Nick Rhea and the monkstables must also be carefully considered. Most certainly, the general public and the media would not be informed. Thus the gap – a welcome breathing space – between lunch and the three o'clock conference was proving valuable because it provided an opportunity, albeit brief, to plan ahead.

When DCS Napier strode into the murder room after lunch, therefore, he approached Detective Inspector Lindsey.

'Come on, Brian, you and I need to talk. We need somewhere we won't be interrupted or overheard.'

'Outside?' suggested DI Lindsey.

'Good idea, there are plenty of seats in the grounds. I have a confession to make.'

'Not you, surely?'

'Yes but mine is to you, not to a priest.'

And so they wandered outside like a pair of old friends chattering about nothing in particular until they reached a bench overlooking the currently deserted cricket field. Bright autumn sunshine flooded the view to highlight the colours of the maturing woodland opposite. The only disruption was a military helicopter taking off nearby, its mission to the Maddleskirk College Cadet Corps complete. Waiting until its sound faded in the distance as it followed the well-used helicopter corridor back to base, and satisfied that their conversation would be totally private, Napier said, 'There's nothing on paper about any of this, Brian. It's far too sensitive. I'll update you on a need-to-know basis and then we'll have to determine how much we can reveal during this investigation. It goes without saying that Operation Rainbow is top secret and currently for your ears only but it does relate to our current murder inquiry as well as the missing monk. I can now tell you the two are linked. This affects the strategy we must adopt.'

'I can keep my mouth shut, boss!'

'I know, so first things first. We have an identity for the murder victim. It has not been revealed to anyone, not even the staff of the murder room. It's not been entered into any of our files and that will be the situation for some time yet. I received the information from the chief constable – he's involved in this. The victim's identification was achieved by fingerprints so there is no doubt about his name even though it's not been officially confirmed. His name is Ian Joseph Radcliffe, he is thirty-two years old and hails from Ealing, one of the London boroughs.'

'So he has convictions? Is this a gangland killing?'

'Partly wrong, Brian. He doesn't have convictions. But his fingerprints are on record.'

'So he's a police officer? *Was* a police officer?'

'Right, and this is a gangland killing. His

mode of death leaves no doubt. As you know, the fingerprints of everyone joining the police are held on record, it's a way of ensuring they behave themselves. So yes, he was a detective inspector from Department C1 of the London Metropolitan Police and he was in this area in an undercover protection role. Now you can see that one serious problem already faces us – we can't make this public and must even keep it from some of our teams.'

'I can understand that. So how did he come to be in that woodland? Here in the peaceful countryside of North Yorkshire? Was it some operation we should have known about?'

'Probably not. He was deep undercover, Brian. I don't know what his cover story is or was, or what false identity he had adopted, but I can tell you that he was involved in the secret supervision and protection of a man who was released from prison on licence some years ago. That operation was so secret that local detectives could not be used in case they were recognized. This detective inspector was drafted in due to problems that affected the released prisoner – he was being targeted by the villain we want to draw into our net. That's our task, Brian, to draw that target man into our net with enough evidence to get him convicted. I can confirm that the murder victim was not known in this area and his presence went virtually unnoticed – exactly what was intended.'

'Obviously somebody *did* find out who he was, and knew why he was here!'

'That's our problem, Brian. Who knew?'

'What do we know about the man he was shadowing?'

'I'm coming to that. His target – a convicted murderer, a man – was sentenced to life imprisonment for the murder of two little girls, twin sisters aged six, in Manchester. He was released on licence after fifteen years inside because it was felt by the parole board that he was no longer a danger to others, especially children. He has been out for about ten years and remains free. On licence, of course.'

'But surely if he was being supervised in such secrecy by a top detective, he must have been considered a danger, despite the parole board's opinions?'

'An alternative view is that he was known to be *in* danger himself, Brian. He was not thought to be a danger to others; others were *known* to be a danger to him.'

'So why wasn't he kept in prison for his own safety?'

'Because he wasn't safe in prison, Brian. He got on the wrong side of a drugs baron by whistle-blowing when he was inside. You know how prisoners treat those who harm children; you can imagine what they would do to a child killer who was also a whistle-blower. He was kept apart, often in solitary confinement for his own safety, but the criminal we are targeting has lieutenants inside most prisons – working on his drugs operations. More about that in due course.'

'No hiding place, in other words?'

'None. But there is something else. There is a strong belief that this particular prisoner was innocent of those murders. He did not kill those little girls.'

'You're saying he was set up for the crimes? This gets curiouser and curiouser...'

'It does, because if that prisoner is innocent, then the evidence points to the girls' stepfather. He is the drug dealer we are targeting and he has emerged as chief suspect for those child murders and other murders. In short, the man who did time for those child murders was framed.'

'Nasty!'

'We're dealing with very brutal and nasty people, Brian. It means that if the released man can persuade the authorities to conduct a cold-case review, his conviction could be quashed and it might be possible to prove the dealer/stepfather killed the children. You might have realized now that our target is actively trying to prevent that cold-case review – it could send him down for a long, long time.'

'And to do that he must eliminate the ex-prisoner? Silence him. Kill him in other words.'

'Right.'

'So it's our task to draw that villain into our net, and get him convicted?'

'That about covers it, Brian.'

'Good God! How did we get involved in this? Here we are, a peaceful rural police force working among beautiful scenery with soothing religious music in this wonderful abbey and now this! So who are we trying to draw into our web? Am I allowed to know?'

'As I said, it's the stepfather of those two little girls. He framed an innocent neighbour, the man who is now out on licence. The stepfather is trying to locate that released prisoner because he knows too much and could get him sent down. DI Radcliffe had been shadowing the ex-prisoner in a protective role whilst trying to secure enough evidence to convict the stepfather of harassment at least. I should add that the stepfather has a known history of violence and drug dealing in a big way as well as other crimes. He shows no mercy to those who cross him. None whatsoever. There are indications he's murdered the children of other rivals. He has always avoided prosecution – through a lack of evidence and no witnesses. But what we know and what we can prove are quite different, Brian.'

'So what's new? Does DI Radcliffe's murder mean that the stepfather has been operating in this area?'

'We've discovered he lives not far away under an assumed name. He's always changing names and addresses; he's dangerous, cunning, clever and rich. Our task in Operation Rainbow is to draw him into our net and get him locked away.'

'Where does the girls' mother fit into all this? Is she still around?'

'She is but I'm sure she had no idea her husband killed her children. We need to find her – it's widely thought she is the brains behind the cover used to conceal the drugs deals. Almost certainly the couple are still together. We believe the girls were killed as an act of revenge against another drug dealer, their real father. It removes his bloodline, that taint has effectively been eliminated ... it tells you a lot about the man we need to draw into our web.'

'You've learned a lot in a short time, sir.'

'It's par for the course, Brian. We never know what a murder investigation will throw up but this is not going to be easy. To be frank, we don't really know how or why Radcliffe turned up dead in that woodland. The forensic examination of his remains and clothing hasn't provided as much evidence as we'd hoped except that he might have died a couple of days before he was found. That brings us to Saturday. However, it's clear

114

from Radcliffe's death that *he* was in danger. Whether his killer knew he was a cop isn't known, but on balance it seems his cover had been blown.'

'With no mercy?'

'None whatever. There is a story that our drug dealer once blew up a rival's house with explosives to kill him. He's that sort of person. He'll stop at nothing to get his own way. It means, Brian, that with DI Radcliffe out of the way, the man he was protecting and watching is all the more vulnerable, especially as he can testify against the villain. That witness is now our responsibility and needs our protection.'

'Do we know who he is?'

'Hereabouts he is known as Father John Attwood.'

'Good grief! The missing monk?'

'The very man.'

'I don't understand all this, boss! You're saying it was our missing monk who was found guilty of killing those two little girls?'

'Yes, that's exactly what I'm saying. When he was released on licence, he was given a new identity and then joined this monastery. The jury had found him guilty but it is now felt, after re-examination of the evidence with an updated forensic input, that the prosecution's case was flawed. The prosecution alleged he had stabbed the girls to death whilst he was supposed to be looking after them. Their real father – turned informer – had been killed in a staged road traffic accident some years earlier. It is now known that the accident was set up to kill him. Their widowed mum was struggling to earn a living whilst looking after them and eventually shacked up with another man. According to the evidence at the trial, our monk was a friend and neighbour of the family. He helped to look after the house and children when the mother and her man-friend, the stepfather, were out.'

'That seems suspiciously like the actions of a paedophile.'

'There was no evidence of that, but it was the prosecution's case that the friendly neighbour – now Father John – cracked and for reasons that have never been explained, slaughtered both girls. Stabbed them umpteen times. Their stepfather was a key witness. That's the basis of this story.'

'So Father John was tried, found guilty and sentenced to life?'

'Yes, two sentences of life imprisonment, running concurrently. In prison, he persistently refused to admit his guilt and so he was not granted parole – but even if he had been granted parole, his record would have followed him.'

'That can happen, sir. Word has a habit of getting out...'

'Or being let out by someone with a

116

motive of some kind! Anyway, once back in the wicked world outside prison, our supposed killer would have suffered in all kinds of ways. As we know, his past would have been made known by those with a big axe to grind, i.e., the girls' surviving relatives. Anyway, to everyone's surprise the convicted killer suddenly admitted his guilt and, after a lot of discussion among those responsible for such things, he was granted parole. It means he is now out on licence with constant checking of his movements and supervision of his mode of living. And to protect him, he has been given a false identity with all the necessary documentation along with a realistic back story. I should tell you that I learned of this only since arriving here. I can't promise I've digested its full import yet. However, I can say it has altered almost everything so far as our investigation is concerned. We now need to re-think our approach in the hope that we'll catch a big fish.'

'There's more to come, isn't there? I can sense it.'

'You're right. There is. Remember I said the name of that missing monk meant something to me? I'd come across it in the course of my work – the force is notified of all such ex-prisoners who live in our patch under new identities.'

'I knew that.'

'Well, our monk is such a man, Brian. Father John Attwood is that child killer who's now out on parole but as you know, he will always be supervised.'

'Freed killers are never really free.'

'They're always subjected to the conditions of their licence. His real name is John Jacobson.'

'With a long criminal record?'

'No. He has no convictions for any other crimes and has never been suspected, not even for paedophilia. Apart from that double murder, his record is squeaky clean, Brian. And he has always protested his innocence; he insists he did not kill those little girls. Now, after all this time, there is doubt about his conviction.'

'But he admitted the crimes to get himself released on licence!'

'With such a high-profile murder on his record, that is the only way he would have been granted parole. It is widely thought he admitted his guilt simply to get out of prison. He intends to establish his innocence but couldn't do so whilst inside.'

'Can I ask if you believe he's innocent?'

'I have no idea, Brian. I've not had chance to study the case in depth, or even read the newspaper reports. With the aid of the internet, we can find out more.'

'So we must reopen his case?'

'On what grounds, Brian? On the say-so of

a man convicted of a very brutal double murder of two children? Our prisons are full of people who claim they are innocent. And another thing, his crimes did not occur in our area, so we don't have ready access to the necessary files. The child murders were in the suburbs of Manchester. If there is to be a cold-case review, it could only be done or initiated by the local police, not us.'

'But surely, in view of our current case, we can ask that force for help? To find out what really happened?'

'We can ask, Brian. That means you've just talked yourself into a job. I would suggest you make an appointment to see the CID boss of Greater Manchester Police immediately if not sooner. Explain your reasons then go and visit him in his office – I'd say the entire case papers will be several feet thick. We don't want an email copy of that lot! You need to speak in person to the officers involved if any are still around. It's possible some are. Try to gauge their gut feeling about the case, ask if there's any chance Attwood alias Jacobson was innocent. I'm sure my counterpart in Greater Manchester will be aware of his release on licence – his department will have been officially notified.'

'I'll get cracking right away. How is this going to affect the way we deal with the present murder?'

'It's not easy to say but we must be somewhat devious from this point onwards. I'm going to suggest we continue our murder enquiries as if we *don't* know the victim's identity. If we release his name, the press will get on to the story and I don't want that kind of sensational revelation, not at this stage. So we keep quiet and continue as if we are trying to ascertain his name, address and personal details. Remember only you and I know the truth. Let's keep it like that for the time being. We can keep our teams and the monk-stables busy trying to find out. It won't be a waste of time because we need to know whether there have been any sightings of him, alone or with a companion. After all, we must know if anyone can throw light on his death. There is still a lot of groundwork to complete.'

'That makes sense; someone must have seen him around here.'

'Our teams can ask whether he's been staying in lodgings or travelling in when necessary. He might have a car parked somewhere. Sooner or later in a rural area like this, it will attract attention.'

'That should keep the local CID and monkstables busy.'

'I'll get them to ask at B&B establishments too. He must have lodged somewhere. We don't need to release his name to achieve a result of this kind but we must try to establish a link with our target villain.'

'So what's the situation with Father John Attwood?'

'He's in great danger but I can tell you he is safe right now. Don't ask how I know – just accept it. Also in his case, there's nothing about his background in our murder room files, although there will be in the CID offices at police headquarters. I suggest we don't release that knowledge at this stage. Let's keep things simple – our line of inquiry is that he's an elderly monk who has vanished and we are concerned for his safety, even if it's on the fringes of a murder inquiry. We are worried about him, that's the official line. In the eyes of the public, that could be due to nothing more than absent mindedness – but someone may have noticed him somewhere. His dog collar and grey suit is a giveaway – if he's still wearing them.'

'So is it possible to keep all this to ourselves? Is it wise?'

'We must keep this to ourselves, at least for the time being, Brian. If news of his disappearance gets into the news media, it could aggravate the risk of others trying to find him. It could generate huge public interest in whether or not he's guilty. We don't want that – not yet anyway. No news is sometimes good news. Now, what about that little monk with specs on? Father Will? He's in the firing line for this crime as well, isn't he? He must be in the frame as a suspect.'

'A suspect? I never thought of him in that light!'

'Well, he must be on our list of suspects or those who need to be proved innocent. Remember he occupied that confessional in place of Father John Attwood, didn't he? And didn't remove Father Attwood's name.'

'I thought he'd not altered the name sign simply because it never occurred to him.'

'He would say that, wouldn't he? And remember the stiletto was found there. We've got to look at things rather more closely now, Brian. We need to know whether he was manning that confessional when the stiletto was placed there, don't we? And if he didn't hide it there, who did?'

'He was in there for an hour on Saturday, starting at six in the evening.'

'Then his presence might be recorded on CCTV footage – except there is a back door into the confessional, the door used by the priests. So maybe he will not show up on that footage?'

'The films are being scrutinized, aren't they?'

'They are but there is more. Suppose we can prove that Father Will was in the confessional when the stiletto was left there. It is almost certain it was used to kill DI Radcliffe and then quickly concealed. We are investigating a murder, remember; everyone is a suspect until proved otherwise. So could

Father Will have used that stiletto to kill the man in the woods sometime that afternoon, and then returned to hide the weapon in the confessional? Concealing it in the folds of his habit?'

'You don't seriously think he's involved, do you, boss?'

'I don't think anything, Brian, I'm trying to find out. But I will say this – there are lots of reasons for having Father Will well and truly in the frame. I think we need to interview him about his movements with precise timings both before and after Radcliffe's murder, if only with the excuse that we are trying to eliminate him from suspicion. So I have lots to do and so do you.'

'I'll get back to the murder room now and ring Manchester.'

'Right. Catch a train from York, do your stuff and you should be back here before midnight. Stay over if you have to. You know your brief – find out as much as you can about John Attwood alias Jacobson, and learn more about the crime he supposedly committed. While you're getting organized, I'll reconstitute my three o'clock conference in view of what we've just discussed but before the conference I will speak to the abbot. I'm not sure how much he knows about Father John Attwood and his past.'

'Or Father Will?'

'All right, I'll ask the abbot about both.

Come along, Brian, there's no time to sit around. I've got to go and see an abbot and you've a train to catch. When you get to Manchester give our best Yorkshire wishes to those folks on the wrong side of the Pennines.'

And so they returned to their respective duties.

Chapter 8

'Father John has been a model of propriety since he joined us,' Abbot Merryman told Napier. 'For a senior citizen with his background, he has settled in remarkably well and has proved most useful when we require any running repairs – he can fix almost anything.'

'I'm interested in his former life, Father Abbot. You are aware of our search for him?'

'Yes, the prior keeps me informed. Any sightings or news?'

'Nothing since he was dropped at Scarborough Beach Hospital at around six on Saturday evening. That's been confirmed. Has he been in contact with you?'

'Sorry, no. Not a word. I find that very odd, Mr Napier. Do you have any idea what's going on? Why would he do such a thing? Why leave here without a word? Then there's that murder in the wood. I do hope he is not involved in that.'

'That has to be considered and I have to question whether he left voluntarily. There are elements to suggest he was tempted away or even tricked into leaving the monastery.'

'So how can I help? We can contact the other British monasteries if that will do any good. He might have sought solace or shelter elsewhere.'

'Anything you can do to trace him will be welcome, Father Abbot.' Napier felt a twinge of guilt in deceiving the abbot in this way but felt it necessary in the circumstances. 'And I need to ask you some questions about him.'

'Clearly you know about his former life?'

'I would never claim to know all about it, Father, but our recent researches have uncovered some unwelcome facts.'

'You're referring to his time in prison for murdering two little girls?'

'Yes, I thought you would be aware of that, but he claims innocence. He's trying to clear his name.'

'He is and I believe in his innocence, Mr Napier. We've had long one-to-one discussions about that awful period of his life and I have no reason to believe he was guilty of those crimes. Here, of course, he is not allowed to teach or work with children but I should add that few if any of our staff or brethren are aware of his past.'

'He confirmed his guilt when he sought to be released on licence.'

'It was a device to secure his freedom, Mr Napier. Don't ask me about the sinfulness of such a manoeuvre, pleading guilty to something he did not do, but he has spent a lot of time in the company of Benedictine monks since he was imprisoned. He was not brought up as a Catholic or in any formal religion, but it was whilst in prison that he befriended one of our monks who regularly visited the jail to celebrate Mass, hear confessions and generally provide solace for the inmates. John attended classes run by our monks. They were not designed to bang on about religion but more to equip the inmates for life outside those four walls. Several monks took turns in hosting the classes, and all came from our Lancashire parishes. Gradually John warmed to our faith and sought to be baptised into the church. He was made very welcome although he was still in prison.

'Then upon his release he joined this monastery and after training became a fully qualified priest/monk. He has told me everything about his past even though I did not make such demands upon him. We don't impose conditions upon our novices and there are times we must accept recruits at face value but in his case I was pleased to learn of his background. Without breaching the seal of confession, Mr Napier, I am convinced of his innocence. In his own words he told me he was "set up" for those crimes. I suspect he meant "framed".'

'Is he seeking revenge?'

'No, his present calling does not embrace revenge, Mr Napier. All he wants is to clear his name. He is a peaceful man and a very good priest and monk.'

'We do hear a lot of prisoners swearing to their innocence, Father Abbot, and we can't investigate every such claim. To be honest, we need more than the word of a convict before an old case can be reopened. We need compelling evidence.'

'I like to think John is different, Mr Napier. I can vouch for him being a very sincere and honest man. So are you able to help him clear his name?'

'That doesn't fall within my terms of reference, Father Abbot, but I'll give him whatever advice I can when we find him. Those murders were not committed within our force area, so Father John will somehow have to persuade the current chief constable of Greater Manchester that there has been a miscarriage of justice within his jurisdiction. That's never easy, convincing anyone that they've made a huge mistake! To set the ball rolling, he'll need supporting evidence of such potency that it will persuade the authorities that he was wrongfully convicted. This needs more than just his word.'

'That's difficult for a man in the later years of life, and without much learning or knowledge of laws, legal procedures and so on. He's a very ordinary man, Mr Napier.'

'My task – our task – is to search and hopefully find him safe and sound, Father Abbot, but we must interview him about the recent murder. It's not to prove his guilt but to prove his innocence. That's my job – to determine the truth. Fortunately, you've all got your feet firmly on the ground!'

'Thank you, Mr Napier, it's good that we can work together. So is there anything I can help with?'

'Two things. If Father John doesn't turn up soon, we'll have to search his room to see whether it contains any clues to his whereabouts. Probably this afternoon.'

'That's not very nice, Mr Napier. We regard a monk's room as a very private place.'

'I agree entirely, but it's necessary. We need something to guide us to wherever he might be. Letters, diaries, notes of some kind. Anything. And the second thing is, what do you know about Father Will Redman?'

'Not a lot. He's a clever man, with a good mathematical brain and knowledge of computers and how they function. Rather shy, I would suggest, and somewhat nervous in a crisis. I'm hoping that being a monkstable will give him more confidence when dealing with people.'

'A brainy man, you'd say?'

'Yes, he's an Oxford graduate and worked in the Bodleian Library before becoming a monk. This abbey has rooms at Oxford University and so, to cut a long story short, he became a novice and is now a trusted member of our community.'

'No hidden agenda then?'

'Nothing like that. Open and honest, a good worker. He has two brothers and a sister who all work in London. He visits them regularly, and he returns their hospitality by letting them stay in our guest room. And, of course, he is one of our monk-constables.'

'I've met him several times during his monkstable duties. However, Father Abbot, I need to eliminate him from our enquiries and that requires some hard questions. You should know that.'

'You mean he's a suspect?' The Abbot sounded horrified.

'He's involved in our enquiries, Father Abbot. He swapped places with Father John at confessions on Saturday, then I found a stiletto in the confessional this morning. It could have been there since the murder. From that fact alone you can understand why I need to interview him. And being close to Father John, he might know more than us about Father John's disappearance and the presence of that dagger. And apart from Tim Farley, your driver, he was the last person to see Father John before he vanished.'

'But Will would never do things like that – murder someone, hide the weapon...'

'Someone has,' said Napier firmly. 'How many friends and families of killers have said that, I wonder? I am not accusing him of anything, Father Abbot. I'm just trying to establish the truth and clarify the situation.'

'Does Will know about this?'

'Not yet, that's my next job. I think he's still on duty in the cop shop as you call it.'

'He enjoys that work, he's in his element in a world of computers and I think he's ideal for that responsibility. He's helping to create a very modern and efficient private police service with first-class communications.'

'I'm sure he's doing a great job. Now one final thing, Father,' continued Napier. 'The murder victim. We have no identification at this stage, and the monkstables are still making enquiries around the campus and local countryside, searching for anyone who might have seen him. Asking at boarding houses, looking for abandoned cars and so on ... they're doing a good job, they're a valuable asset to the inquiry. You should be pleased with them.'

'I am, and thank you.'

And so Detective Chief Superintendent Napier left the abbot's office and headed for the cop shop where Father Will was still working.

'Mr Napier, how nice to see you,' said Father Will. 'How can I help?'

'I need to talk to you for about twenty minutes or so. Is there somewhere we can go without being disturbed?'

'There's the abbey's guest lounge, it's usually empty about now. I'll just call Prior Tuck to let him know the shop is not staffed.' He locked the door and led the big man through the abbey church and out into a separate area that contained several small rooms. Will smiled and led him into the one marked 'Lounge'.

'Take a seat.'

'Thanks, Father Will.' Napier settled down at the table. 'Now, I'm sure you're wondering why I need to talk to you, but this is important. It's concerning the murder of the man in Ashwell Priory woods. I must stress you are not under suspicion but I need to eliminate you from our enquiries.'

'You can't think I did it? Surely...' The monk's voice developed a distinct tremor.

'I don't think anything, Father Will. My task is to find out. Now I'm interested in you because you swapped places with Father John at confession time. As you are surely aware, we're still looking for him.'

'Yes, I know, it is most strange. Where can

he be?'

'We need to find out, so please tell me everything about that exchange of duties, with as much detail as possible.'

'Well, it was nothing out of the ordinary; all of us swap duties from time to time. He came to see me on Saturday afternoon, just before five, and asked if I would take confession at six in his place. I said it was no problem and I'd be pleased to help – that was from six until seven.'

'Did he tell you why?'

'Yes, he said he'd had a phone call from Scarborough Beach Hospital asking him to go there as soon as possible because the consultant had found something in a recent sample that required a face-to-face discussion. He has prostate cancer but is coping with it. The caller asked Father John to visit the hospital at six that evening when the specialist would speak to him.'

'Was he told anything about that finding?'

'Only that it was associated with his prostate cancer diagnosis some months earlier.'

'Did a man or a woman call him?'

'A woman, she said she worked on reception but didn't give a name.'

'Did he check the call? Ring back? Query it in any way?'

'No, he didn't argue. He has been receiving treatment for prostate cancer so the call wasn't unusual. The woman said she couldn't

132

discuss it over the phone. If he had any queries, he should discuss them with his consultant.'

'Did she suggest he may have to be an in-patient, perhaps just overnight?'

'No, he asked but she said no. He would be free to come home immediately after the consultation.'

'And then?'

'Well, I agreed to take his turn at six o'clock confessions and he booked one of the official cars to take him to the hospital, leaving here at five o'clock.'

'A single journey?'

'There was talk of the driver waiting for him but John said he didn't want him hanging around for an indefinite period. He said he would find his own way home – taxi, perhaps, or a bus.'

'Did he say anything to you before he left?'

'No, he was in a rush. I bade him farewell and good wishes, and off he went. He said he'd update me when he got back.'

'And then what happened?'

'I went to the confessional box at about ten to six and settled down. It's a regular weekly session, usually well attended. That evening there was a steady stream of penitents until seven o'clock. You know I can't reveal anything they told me, Mr Napier. The seal of confession is absolute.'

'I've learned a lot about that since I came

here. So did anything unusual happen during your spell of duty?'

'No, nothing.' Napier caught the nervous glance in Father Will's eyes.

'Nobody confessed to a murder then?' Napier produced a thin smile.

'I am not allowed to break the seal of confession. I can't answer such a question.'

'I'm not asking you to reveal the identity of such a person, if indeed it did happen. I'm just asking whether such a thing occurred.'

'I cannot break the seal of confession, Mr Napier. I want to help your enquiries in any way possible, but that is one thing I cannot and must not do.'

'Did you know that someone left a stiletto dagger in the confessional? Hidden under the kneeler?'

'I know nothing about that, Mr Napier, please God I do not.'

'Early forensic tests indicate it is the weapon that killed the man in the wood. There are traces of his blood on the blade near the hilt, missed when somebody tried to clean it ... but we don't know where this weapon has come from or who left it there. It will be subjected to further forensic examinations but there were no fingerprints.'

'I'm sorry I can't help, really I can't...'

'So no one confessed to using this weapon, did they? Before they left it in your confessional?'

'I had no idea it was there, Mr Napier, no idea at all. Most definitely not. I did not put it there and I have no idea who did. Truly I haven't.'

'I noticed you didn't change Father John's name-board before the confessions. Was that deliberate? Or did you want the penitents to think they were speaking to Father John?'

'I never gave it a thought, Mr Napier, not once. I didn't see the name-board because I entered through the back door.'

'So then what happened once time was up?'

'I left the confessional and went to my room to prepare for Vespers.'

'So you didn't check the confessional to see whether anyone had left anything?'

'No, the cleaners do that.'

'How often?'

'I don't know, probably once a week. There's always confessions on a Saturday evening at six for an hour, so I guess the cleaners tidy things up on Friday at the latest.'

'And when you left the confessional, was there any message from Father John to explain his absence?'

'Nothing. Well, not to me. I don't know whether he rang anyone else.'

'If he had rung to say he would not be returning, who would he talk to?'

'Probably Prior Tuck. If not, it would be the abbot.'

'Now, you realize there are closed circuit TV cameras in the abbey church? They were running when those confessions were underway so we can see who attended, and at what time. So can I ask you again, were you aware that anyone had hidden a dagger under the kneeler?'

'No, if I had known, I'd have recovered it and taken it to reception.'

'Not the police?'

'We have our procedures, lots of strange things get left in the confessional. We lodge them at Reception because you can be sure the losers will come back sooner or later. And there was no reason at that stage to think that dagger had been involved in a killing.'

'Perhaps it's a good thing you didn't hand it to the police! At least we have it in our custody. You can see why I'm interested in someone who might have confessed to murder before ridding themselves of the evidence. You can probably understand why this makes me believe you might have heard someone confess to murder.'

'I've told you, Mr Napier, and I repeat, the seal of confession is absolute.' Father Will's voice was quivering with emotion.

'So are you the killer? I have to ask you that, it is my duty. Did you stab the man in the wood, then come here before confessions to hide the weapon and probably implicate someone else?'

'Oh dear God, how can you think such a thing, Mr Napier?'

'Because it is my job to think such a thing, Father Will. And if I think you are involved, I shall need to formally caution you...'

'This is dreadful...'

'Either you have been well and truly framed or you are sheltering a murderer. I may need to ask you more questions but not yet. Meanwhile I shall go away and think about all this. We'll talk again. I am always available if you need to discuss this further...'

Chapter 9

When Detective Chief Superintendent Napier returned to the murder room, it was buzzing with activity. Detectives, men and women, seemed to be everywhere, all chattering and renewing old acquaintances. Many had worked together on previous murders and major investigations. Arrivals from around the county were logged in, as well as Nick and the monkstables, and all were asked to update themselves with the progress of the investigation. The information was available from computers, whiteboards, blackboards and even leaflets already rushed out by computer. In temporary charge during Inspector Lindsey's absence was Detective Sergeant Jane Salkeld, a capable officer.

'Anything to report, Sarge?' asked Napier as he strode in.

'Most of our teams have reported in, sir, so we'll be on target for the 3 p.m. team conference. You'll be pleased to know we've just received some useful data from the CCTV cameras in the abbey church. Prior Tuck has managed to glean it from the monitors and records in reception. It's interesting.'

'Then I'd better see it. Where is he?'

'With that viewing cabinet over there.' She pointed to the structure that looked like a fruit machine. Napier grunted his appreciation and strode across.

'Ah, Friar Tuck, we have a modest success, I understand.'

'We have, Mr Napier. I can show you – I've got the tapes on this machine. They're a wee bit blurred but they do provide the gist of events during Saturday confessions.'

'Even without any spoken words?'

'Yes, there's no sound but that's always top secret anyway,' said the prior, now accustomed to Napier's use of the word Friar.

'So I'm constantly being told but I keep trying. You realize the identity of the killer might have been revealed during those confessions. I find that very frustrating. I never get people confessing as readily as that.'

'But some offenders do confess to their crimes?' suggested the prior.

'Not to me they don't. Most say nowt because they know their right to remain silent even if I know their wrongdoings. It's reliable evidence that convicts them, not confessions. And we do get people falsely confessing to murder. Anyway, enough of that. Show me what you've got.'

With Napier at his side, Prior Tuck showed the Saturday tape, explaining that each tape was renewed daily at 5 a.m. by the duty monk, and each ran for twenty-four hours. A clock on the machine confirmed that it was showing Saturday's events.

Then Prior Tuck halted the tape at twelve noon. 'I'm showing you this to focus on that woman who's just come from one of the pews near the confessional.'

'Why her?'

'Because the same woman appears later, going into the confessional box when Father Will was hearing confessions. His first customer. Not long after six o'clock.'

'Was she, by jove! Slow the film down, we need a good look at her. Fair hair, a tan jumper and greenish jeans. Any idea who she is?'

'Not at the moment, but we've not shown this film to anyone else – it's just come in.'

'Can we print stills from it?'

'The computer department can do that.'

'You've a computer department?'

'It's for college students studying information technology, but the tutors have the
necessary expertise and equipment to print
stills from this tape.'

'You want for nothing here! Keep going.'

The film, speeded up temporarily, showed
the ongoing scene in the south transept.
Many of the people in the film were identified by the prior as members of staff just
passing through, although some were on
retreat courses and others were day visitors.
They entered the camera's range, looked
around and departed without exciting any
interest in the viewers. Then Prior Tuck
stopped again.

'There she is again, Mr Napier. A wee bit
clearer this time. Same clothing as before. A
tan jumper and greenish jeans. Autumn
wear. It was a warm September day. She's of
medium build, fair hair, worn short. Age?
Dunno...'

'Late forties I'd guess,' said Napier. 'Give
or take a year or so. Maybe into her fifties.
So what time was this taken?'

'Half past three on Saturday afternoon.
Now watch her. She's alone in that part of
the church.'

After looking at some of the statues and
wall paintings, the woman went across to
the confessional and read the noticeboards.

One of them gave the times of confession, but even with this poor image, they could see the name on the board above it, in larger letters. It was Father John Attwood's name-board. Then she opened the door of the confessional and peered inside. By holding it open, the dim light remained on. She held the door wide open and then, using her foot, reached forward to kick the kneeler. It moved without constraint. Using her foot again she restored it to its former position, closed the door and moved away.

At that point, a man and woman entered the south transept and so the woman slid into a pew and knelt down as if in prayer.

Prior Tuck resumed his commentary. 'She stayed there for a few minutes as the new-comers entered but she never spoke to them, and then she left. She does not appear again until about five past six that same evening. There's no doubt it is the same woman. On that occasion she goes straight into a pew to await her turn for confession. We've caught that on camera too. First in the queue with about eight people waiting. She doesn't acknowledge any of them.'

'Do we know who they are?' asked Napier. 'I'd like to talk to them, so see whether any of them know this woman.'

'It's doubtful, Mr Napier. The abbey church is not like a parish church where you get the same people turning up time and time again, except of course for the students – they're regular attenders. Even so, this place tends to cater more for visitors with lots of different churchgoers each weekend or even each weekday. Also, many of the staff go home after work and not many work on Saturdays, except the domestic staff in the college area. The chances are that most of those people are strangers to one another.'

'That could be why this woman selected it,' suggested Napier. 'So she wouldn't be recognized. But we must trace and question them, if we can find them. One of them might know her. That's all it takes, just one.'

'I can ask around the campus and show pictures of her,' suggested Prior Tuck. 'We could get the monkstables to do that – Nick will guide them. Someone might have seen her or even given her accommodation nearby. And she might have arrived by car – there's a lot we need to find out.'

Prior Tuck moved the film forward to show the woman's arrival and then focused on her taking her place in the queuing area.

'What's she carrying?' Napier leaned forward to obtain a clearer image of the moving woman. 'Reverse it. Friar Tuck ... take us to when she enters this time, slow it down ... I want to see what she's carrying. It's not a handbag, is it? Now is that curious? A woman without a handbag?'

'I'm not very *au fait* with women and their

handbag-carrying customs! Would she bring her handbag to confession? Surely she'd leave it somewhere safe.'

'She's a woman, Friar Tuck. She'd probably have it with her and she'd take great care not to leave it anywhere. Although this woman hasn't a handbag, she does have an umbrella, one of those large ones you see at race meetings and events like golf matches. With blue and white stripes. Furled.'

'Is that what it is?'

'I think so even if the image is rather blurred. Now why would a woman bring a huge colourful umbrella to confession on a fine September day – it was a fine day, if you recall. So, can you think of anything better for concealing and carrying a stiletto dagger? Much more practical and secretive than a rolled-up newspaper.'

'Now that you mention it, it does seem ideal. I'll fast forward until she gets up from the pew to enter the confessional.'

As they watched that section, they saw the woman stand up when her turn came. She walked from the pew towards the confessional box, carrying the umbrella not by its handle but with her right hand gripping it around the folds, holding them tightly together midway along its length. She opened the door with her free hand and stepped inside as the door closed behind her to extinguish its modest light. The time was seven minutes past six.

'I need to talk to Father Will again,' said Napier. 'He must have heard something odd as she extricated the stiletto from the umbrella and shoved it under the kneeler.'

'She was in there less than five minutes,' said Prior Tuck. 'Here she comes again, leaving the confessional but carrying her brolly by its handle. She didn't return to the pew to say her prayers neither did she remain in church but left the building just before quarter past. So far as we know, she was never seen again inside the abbey church. I don't know where she went from there.'

'Then we must find out,' muttered the indefatigable Napier. 'Someone must have seen her outside the abbey church.'

Prior Tuck switched off the machine. 'We can run this through again and again if necessary. It might help.'

'We'll need to see it again, especially Nick and the monkstables, if they're to continue local enquiries. And I think Father Attwood's driver should have a look at that woman.' Napier was thinking aloud. 'So the big question is this – did she leave the stiletto in the confessional? If so, how far had she carried it in the brolly? And where from? Once more, she might have been noticed by someone. Those monkstables need to ask a lot of questions around the campus.'

'A lot depends on how she arrived at the abbey church,' was the prior's response. 'There's no parking immediately outside and the visitors' car park is several blocks away. Someone might have noticed her, especially carrying such a colourful brolly, and wondered why she wanted it on such a mild and dry day.'

'It seems we're going to keep your monk-stables busy,' said Napier, beaming.

'I've worked with less efficient police officers,' admitted the prior.

'Right. Well, Friar Tuck, it stands to reason that somebody must have seen her around these premises. Where did she come from? Had she been walking in those woods at any time? If she was, did she stumble across the stiletto? Did she find it and decide to take it with her, wherever she was going? Then changed her mind and got rid of it? Did she have a vehicle and if so was someone waiting for her outside the abbey church? There are many, many questions to be asked – and answered.'

'There's something else to consider,' Prior Tuck suggested. 'If this woman arrived at this confessional just after six o'clock, she could *not* be the same one who greeted Father Attwood outside Scarborough Beach Hospital just before six. There are similarities in their appearance but there is no way she could have travelled the thirty miles or so from Scarborough in those few minutes. Clearly we are looking for two women. We have a description of the Scarborough woman on file, provided by the abbey driver.'

'Good point, Friar! And did the Scarborough woman have a mobile? Could she have called Father John? We need the driver to look at these photos when we get them organized. He might recognize her, might be able to point us in her direction even with a name or some other form of identification. We must consider and examine every probability. Maybe these two women are completely unknown to each other? We mustn't be sidetracked by distracting evidence. Remember, the disappearance of Father John might not be linked in any way to the murder but I'm not one for believing in coincidence in such cases, Friar Tuck. You as an ex-copper should know that.'

'Which is why I mentioned it,' said Prior Tuck, smiling.

'Right, keep a tight rein on that film. We need to make much wider use of it, but now it's almost time for the CID conference. I'd like all your troops there.'

'It's already been arranged.'

'Splendid. And if I deal with the murder in the wood, can you cope with the disappearance of Father John?'

'Of course.'

'Then I've just time for another chat with

Father Will. Whatever he can tell us will be rich fodder for the conference. So see you later.'

When Napier returned to the cop shop, Father Will was about to close it so that he could attend the CID conference.

'I'm just leaving for the conference,' said the quiet monk. 'Is it important, Mr Napier?'

'Important enough to be sorted out before we both attend the conference, Father Will.'

'I do hope you are not going to try and pressure me again into revealing the contents of the confessions.'

'No, I'm not, but it's associated with that. I'm concerned about the confessional box itself rather than its customers.'

'You'd better come in. I can lock the door to keep it private.'

When they were settled, Napier spoke quietly. 'I know I've put you under some pressure, Father Will, and I'm sorry to have to question you again.'

'You have to do your job, like us all.'

'How true. Father, please try to be frank and helpful with me. Since we last spoke, we have discovered some footage on the CCTV security tapes that cover the confessional and south transept.'

As Napier described what those extracts had revealed, Father Will listened in silence.

'At a few minutes past six, Father Will, a woman, perhaps in her late forties or early

147

fifties, casually dressed in a tan top and green jeans, entered the confessional during your tenure. She was your first penitent.'

'You know I cannot discuss this...'

'Please hear me out, Father. Earlier in the day, she had been filmed examining the interior of the confessional, moving the kneeler around with her foot.'

'Goodness me! Why would she do that?'

'That is what we want to know. Now, when she went back there to make her confession, she was filmed entering the confessional whilst carrying a large blue and white umbrella.'

'People bring all sorts with them ... and often leave things behind.'

'Now I don't know everything that goes on in one of those tight little boxes but I would imagine a woman with a large brolly would have difficulty finding somewhere to put it especially as, when the door closes, the interior is in darkness.'

'There is a kneeler, Mr Napier, fairly low, in fact. Some people have to move that to get settled, especially a large person following a smaller one who'd probably shift it around a little.'

'I am leading up to that. So did that woman, your first customer on that occasion, appear to have trouble getting settled? On her knees with a large brolly to battle with? In the darkness?'

'I'll be honest with you, Mr Napier. She did appear to have difficulty settling down. I attributed it to the darkness and perhaps because she was a stranger. I wondered if she was carrying shopping or something.'

'Could you recognize any of the sounds she was making?'

'No, I couldn't see what she was carrying either: one cannot see much from the other side of the grille in those boxes.'

'But she was struggling to settle down?'

'I'd say so, yes, just a little. And I am not breaking the seal of confession by telling you that. She had not begun at that stage.'

'When she finished, Father, she emerged and took the umbrella with her. But we have reason to believe she left something behind, quite deliberately. The stiletto dagger that had been concealed and smuggled inside within the folds of her umbrella.'

'Oh dear God, whatever next! I cannot comment. I know nothing about that. I never saw her do such a thing. She never mentioned it. Could she have lost it? Slipped out of the umbrella without her knowing? The stiletto, I mean?' Father Will now appeared to be extremely nervous, licking his lips and avoiding eye contact with Napier.

'We don't think so. We think she deliberately disposed of it because it was the weapon used to kill the man in the wood. Did it belong to her, or had she found it?'

149

Father Will paused and issued a huge sigh with almost a sobbing sound, 'Mr Napier, I know nothing of that. Absolutely nothing. Truly I do not.'

'I believe you. That has settled one small matter so let's continue our normal routine. It's time to attend the conference.'

Chapter 10

After welcoming his newly arrived officers and introducing Nick and the monkstables, Detective Chief Superintendent Napier dealt with minor details such as hours of work, expenses, overtime and murder room discipline. Then he outlined the key facts of the murder. Quite deliberately, he concealed the name and profession of the victim. That was for later.

'You'll be allocated your actions by Detective Sergeant Salkeld. She is standing in for Detective Inspector Lindsey who is making enquiries in Lancashire. He is following what could be a strong line of inquiry that may or may not be associated with this murder. That's for me to decide. More about that in due course. Our immediate concern is to get the murder victim identified and establish sightings of him. His details are displayed on the blackboard and there are colour photographs of the body at the scene of the murder. Take a good look then get out there to get him identified, trace his movements and establish his contacts. Somebody will know him, somebody must have seen him around. Has he a car? A motorbike? A pedal bike? Is there such a vehicle abandoned nearby? In one of the local villages? Where has he been staying? Does he have friends and contacts here? A woman friend? A backpack abandoned?

'Two women might be involved. The first is shown on a CCTV security film of the church interior – have a word with Detective Constable Sheila Trowbridge over there.' He pointed to her. 'She'll show you extracts from the film, as many as you want, and she can arrange prints – they're always useful if you find a witness who may have seen her. We believe that woman concealed a stiletto dagger in the confessional and we're sure it's the murder weapon. Bear that in mind.

'But did she kill that man in the wood or is she merely an accessory? Whatever role she played, we need to find her. We know she was on this campus around six o'clock on Saturday evening in the abbey church, the cameras tell us that. She was carrying a large folded blue and white umbrella. On a warm sunny day with not a spot of rain. Who is she? How did she get here? Someone must have seen her. Someone might have spoken to her. Was she sighted together with the murder victim anywhere near those woods? That's an important point – I don't believe his body was carried up into those woods and dumped, that would be impossible due to the location. It suggests he was killed close to where he was found. Probably with a stiletto type of dagger. Where did it come from? The PM revealed a lot of broken bones, probably happening after death. So was his body thrown from the cliff? If so, who by? You need to find out if anyone else was in those woods at the time. Don't ignore the victim but do concentrate on that woman. Has she been staying locally with friends, in digs or a hotel? Has she been seen in that wood? We need to identify her and bring her in for questioning. Any questions so far?'

There were no questions but he knew they would arise as their enquiries generated more evidence and more puzzles. He allowed them a few moments to consider his words then said, 'Let me remind you – this murder has several key elements. First, who is the deceased and who killed him? Second, who is that woman and what role did she play? Third – what is the motive? If we can answer those, we shall be on the way to resolving this case. Now, I'm going to introduce the prior of Maddleskirk Abbey to explain something which may or may not be associated with this murder. If you ask my opinion about a probable connection, I will say I have an open mind. Friar Tuck, the floor is yours.'

Prior Tuck, a rounded, cheerful monk of some fifty years, stood up, smiling at Napier's continued reference to him as Friar Tuck.

'I am Prior Gabriel Tuck which means I am the deputy abbot, and among my varied duties, I'm in charge of the monkstables gathered here. If you ask the question as to my qualification for that duty, I am a former police officer with twenty-five years' experience and I have worked on several murder investigations. On Saturday evening, one of our senior monks, Father John Attwood, went missing.' He then explained in considerable detail the known facts, reinforcing the mystery of Father John's summons to hospital. 'The question we must all ask ourselves is this – has his disappearance any connection with the murder of that man in the wood? Are we conducting two enquiries, or just one? With Mr Napier's agreement, our efforts to trace Father John will, for the time being, run separately from the murder enquiry.'

Napier interrupted. 'There must be a voluntary cross-fertilization of ideas and an exchange of evidence that could link both investigations. There are certain facts that must be established as separate issues and the monkstables are in an ideal situation for finding their missing monk. Once the facts are clearer, we may have to merge the two investigations. Already, as you have just heard from Friar Tuck, there are several linking pieces of evidence. Bear these in mind as you undertake your actions but don't be afraid to explore your own ideas or ask for advice. We need hard-working brains on this.'

'Thanks, Mr Napier,' responded Prior Tuck. 'One thing to consider is that I have shown to Tim Farley, the driver who took Father Attwood to hospital, several print-outs of the woman on the church CCTV film. He does not know her but expressed a view she was similar in age and appearance to the woman he saw greet Father Attwood at Scarborough Beach Hospital but sadly she was in the shadows.'

'Keep digging, Friar Tuck. I'm still not sure whether we're talking about one woman or two.'

Nick Rhea, sitting quietly among the monkstables, raised his hand and reminded them, 'We know, of course, it could not be the same woman who entered the confessional. The distance and time involved rules out that possibility. So we do need to trace and identify both. I should remind you that the woman in the CCTV film of the abbey church interior was not carrying a handbag.

That's odd, so where was it? Just outside in her car? It sounds possible so we need to find that car. Someone on the campus must have seen it – and her.'

'Thanks, Nick, so where do we go from here?' asked Prior Tuck. 'Brother George?'

'Here!' A grey-haired monk raised his hand.

Brother George was not an ordained priest but was a monk and also one of the monkstables. A senior monk by age alone, he preferred the outdoor life and would rather spend time in this vegetable patch than sing hymns in the abbey choir.

The prior addressed him. 'We know you keep a record of registration numbers of almost every vehicle that enters these grounds, so perhaps you noted this woman's car? If she had one, that is. It would probably be somewhere in the grounds on Saturday afternoon, particularly just before six o'clock and until about half past or even later. Indeed it might have been parked outside the south door despite the restrictions. And did some of those other penitents arrive by car? If so, where did they park? Did they notice the woman without a handbag but carrying a blue and white rolled umbrella? We need to find them and interview them to determine whether they noticed the mystery woman, or even knew who she was.'

'I'll check my lists, Father Prior.'

'Thank you. Mr Napier, back to you,' said Prior Tuck.

'Right, well, that's it. Off you all go. We will have a round-up conference here at six o'clock to pool our knowledge before we disperse. There will be late shift in the murder room until 11 p.m. and then a night duty detective inside the room until 6 a.m.'

When Detective Chief Superintendent Napier dismissed the teams to go about their enquiries, Prior Tuck reminded his monkstables to return to the Postgate Room for their full briefing and allocation of actions. He turned to Nick Rhea. 'Coming with us, Nick? Or is your spell with us now over?'

'I don't want to get in the way but if I can help, I will,' offered Nick.

'Your help is always appreciated. We're still amateurs at this sort of thing. I see we haven't the pleasure of the company of Oscar Blaketon and Alf Ventress this time?'

'I doubt if news of these events will have reached them – there's been nothing in the news – but once that happens, I don't think they'll be able to keep away!'

'We can always use their experience. Now, is there any particular line of enquiry you think we should follow?'

'There's one I would like to pursue in person right now, Prior Tuck, but it's more associated with the murder inquiry than our hunt for Father John.'

'I'll happily go along with that but should you mention it to Mr Napier?'

'Not immediately. I need another chat with Barnaby Crabstaff first, and he said he was heading off for a meeting with Claude Jeremiah Greengrass. I thought I might catch him at Claude's emporium. I just want to see if Barnaby knows more than he's told us so far, and if he does I'll pass it on to Mr Napier's teams.'

'But you'll keep in touch? To be honest, Nick, we need you here.'

'I'll return once I've talked to Barnaby.'

'And we'll get busy around the campus.'

Claude Jeremiah Greengrass lived at Hagg Bottom, Aidensfield, and his emporium could be seen from afar, being instantly recognizable due to its conglomeration of rusting ironware, old agricultural machinery, derelict tractors, bicycle parts and almost any other thing that had generated, or could generate, scrap metal. There was a lot of discarded woodwork too, such as old wardrobes, chests of drawers, chairs and tables.

Nick, who as the village bobby of Aidensfield had often had cause to visit this place, was familiar with the tracks through the mountain of debris and so made his way to what Claude called his office. It was an

157

old caravan with no wheels but equipped with a stove that burned wood, coal and almost anything else Claude put inside it; there were occasions when the stench from the chimney was so strong and unpleasant that neighbours living downwind complained. Claude always blamed the coal merchant.

Nick rapped on the open door and peered inside. Claude and Barnaby were both there, seated at the table with mugs of coffee before them as they pored over what appeared to be a map.

'Now then, Claude, can I come in?'

'Oh my Gawd, whatever do you want, Constable Rhea? I thought I was going to have a period of peace and calm now that you've retired and left Aidensfield. Look, whatever it is, it wasn't my fault, I didn't do it and neither did my mate here. We're innocent, both of us.'

'We're both innocent,' chanted Barnaby.

'I'm not a policeman any more, Claude.'

'Mebbe not, but you make a good imitation of one, snooping around my yard like a tax inspector.'

Nick continued inside and pulled out a chair to settle at their table.

'Is it a coffee you want?'

'No, Claude, I had one before I set off, thanks.' Nick didn't fancy one of Claude's dirty mugs. 'I'm here about that body found in the woods.'

'It was nowt to do with me, Constable Rhea.'

'Or me,' echoed Barnaby.

'I realize that but I thought you might be able to help.'

'Help the police? Me? You must be joking!'

'I thought you might help the family of the dead man, Claude.'

'Aye, well, that's different. So what are you asking?'

'First, do you know who he is?'

'No idea,' said Claude.

'No idea,' added Barnaby.

'Did you see him around here, before he was attacked?'

'I might have done...'

'He might have done...'

'Might you?' Nick pulled a photo of the dead man from his pocket. It was taken on the mortuary slab, with his body covered with a white sheet to leave his facial features on show. 'Mid thirties, white skin, dark hair, slim build, wearing a dark green T-shirt, blue jeans and white plimsolls. Not hiking gear, Claude, but casual enough to be on holiday. We need sightings of him, we need to get him named.'

'Well, he might have been here...'

'If he was, Claude, we need to know whether he was here alone or whether he had anyone with him.'

'Do I get a reward if I tell you?'

'Do we get a reward?' asked Barnaby.

'Just the reward of knowing you've done some good service for the benefit of your fellows and the community, Claude and Barnaby. So I repeat, did either of you see him before he died?'

'Then yes, Constable Rhea, I did see him.'

'He saw him, Mr Rhea.'

'When and where?'

'Up near the pond, the old wishing well, he was up there just looking around.'

'When was this?'

'Middle of last week, I'd say. Wednesday or Thursday. On a morning.'

'Can you be more precise?'

'Elevenish, mebbe, give and take a bit.'

'It was definitely a Wednesday, Claude,' volunteered Barnaby.

'It was. He's right,' admitted Claude.

'Alone, was he?'

'No, there was a woman with him. A bit older than him, not old enough to be his mother by my reckoning. Might have been an older sister or summat. Young aunt ... mature girlfriend ... you can make up all sorts of things out of that, can't you?'

'It's always possible, Claude. Now this is good news and extremely interesting. Did you know her?'

'No, she's not local, I can tell you that.'

'How do you know?'

'Well, she didn't speak like a local, she sounded like a foreigner from Lancashire to me.'

'You heard her?'

'I was hiding in the bushes, Constable. I didn't want anybody to see me there in case they thought I was poaching. I can disappear like magic in undergrowth and bushes, become totally invisible. It's easy when you know how.'

'Were you poaching?'

'No, I was not! There's nowt in that pond anyway, no fish to speak of...'

'So tell me what you saw.'

'It was just a couple going for a walk, I didn't take much interest. You do see couples walking up there, you know, being St Valentine's Well, all very romantic. I don't go around spying on people, I'm not that depraved.'

'Did they appear romantic? Holding hands? Kissing? That sort of thing.'

'No, nothing like that. They looked like a businessman discussing business with a female colleague, not at all lovey-dovey.'

'From your hiding place, could you hear what they were saying?'

'No, not a chance. They were too far away, speaking in soft voices.'

'Now, can you describe her?'

'Well, I didn't take a lot of notice...'

'Claude, I know you from the past. You've

a sharp eye, you're observant and you're always interested in what goes on around you. That's why you are such a successful businessman. I am sure you noticed something about her.'

'He's a very successful businessman, is Mr Greengrass.'

'Not young,' said Claude. 'Not as young as the lad she was with. Middle into her forties, I'd say. Well into them as a matter of fact. I'm not very good at guessing women's ages, Mr Rhea, but she was older than him. Dressed in summer gear. It was a lovely warm September morning.'

'Summer gear?'

'Jeans. Light green jeans and a light brown top of some sort. Fair hair, short and rather curly.'

'Was she carrying anything? Camera? Hiking stick? Haversack?'

'Nothing. She was empty handed. Not even a handbag. It's not often you see women out and about without a handbag of some kind, is it?'

'Definitely not,' Nick agreed.

'Definitely not,' added Barnaby.

'So how had they got there? Together? Did they arrive separately? Were cars involved? Or other transport?'

'I've no idea, Mr Rhea, I just happened to be up there when I heard them chattering as they came towards St Valentine's Well, so I did my usual trick and vanished into the bushes. That's survival instinct, Mr Rhea. I'm good at evasive action, disappearing when trouble might be on its way. Keeping out of bother.'

'So then what happened? Did you show yourself?'

'No, I did not! I had a meeting down in Elsinby at the far side of the pond, so I waited until they'd gone, then I continued my way to Elsinby, down through that woodland away from the Maddleskirk entrance. They would never know I'd seen them and they would not have seen me.'

'What about you, Barnaby? Did you see them at the pond?'

'No, Mr Rhea, I only saw the man when I found him like I told you, but he was dead by then. I never saw the woman, so I did not.'

'Claude.' Nick looked him in the eyes. 'This is vitally important to the murder inquiry. You need to repeat this to Detective Chief Superintendent Napier, just as you've told it to me. And look at a photograph from the abbey CCTV. I will relate what you've said, but he'll need to hear it from you.'

He screwed up his eyes, and twisted his head around as if his neck was hurting. Nick knew he was going through agonies at the idea of having to help the police.

'Will there be a reward?' he asked. 'Did I

ask that?'

'You did and there isn't, but your co-operation will be noted in police circles. That might do you some good in the future.'

'You're not trying to bribe me, are you?'

'Would I dare, Claude! So can I tell Mr Napier where to find you?'

'I'll be here for the next day or two – me and Barnaby are sorting out the good stuff from the bad. I'm going to have a big sale. Sale of the century.'

'It'll be the sale of the century,' added Barnaby.

'Then you'll need publicity? Maybe I could reward you by offering to publicize your enterprise?'

'Now you're talking, Mr Rhea. This sounds like a very businesslike proposition.'

'It's a very businesslike proposition, Mr Rhea,' said Barnaby.

'This could set me on the road to my first million, couldn't it? All right, Mr Rhea, tell that detective chap he can come and talk me here.'

'I will, and thanks, Claude. You've no idea how important this is to the inquiry.'

'Aye, well, we do our best to help the constabulary when they're in great need ... just as I'm in great need now of earning some extra cash.'

'Good deeds are always rewarded, Claude.'

'Not in my world, they're not, but I do keep trying. Just tell that detective I'll talk to him.'

Chapter 11

After listening to Nick's account, Detective Chief Superintendent Napier lost no time in heading for the Greengrass ranch to interview Claude. Meanwhile Nick remained in the Postgate Room for an hour or so before going home; he wanted to check the value of the information the monkstables had gathered. Some of it may prove of interest to the murder room teams; Nick would act as intermediary.

As both enquiries were settling into their momentum, Detective Inspector Brian Lindsey arrived at the headquarters of Greater Manchester Police. The force headquarters had recently moved into a new state-of-the-art building at Newton Heath, to the north of the city.

The clerk at reception asked for confirmation of his identity then inspected his warrant card before ringing the CID offices to announce his presence. He was then told that Detective Chief Inspector Hammond was expecting him and she would come down to escort him up to her office, complete with his 'Authorised Visitor' name-badge. She was a tall dark-haired young woman in her early forties, slim and elegant with dark hair and a ready smile. She was smartly dressed in a dark navy jacket and skirt, white shirt and black shoes and exuded an air of calm efficiency. He thought she looked more like a business executive than a senior detective.

'Hi.' She extended her hand for him to shake. 'I'm DCI Pauline Hammond, Mr Lindsey. Call me Pauline.'

'I'm Brian,' he told her.

'Follow me, I've a pot of tea and cakes organized in my office – they'll help after your journey. You'll be pleased that I've found the file you want to examine. I must tell you that this crime happened before I joined the force so I hope I can help.'

'I'm sure it will be useful,' was all he could think of saying as he followed her into the lift and up to the second floor.

'In here.' She opened a door and showed him into her smart office with extensive views across the city. It contained her desk as well as a small conference table with six chairs.

'Take a seat,' she invited, indicating a chair at the table and joining him as she organized the tea and cakes. A thick file waited on the table.

'This is very civilized!' He sat down and placed his briefcase on the table.

'It's our new home, Brian. We enjoy working here, it's a massive improvement after our previous old-fashioned offices at Chester House. We can even invite visitors to have tea and cakes! It's the Jacobson murders that interest you, am I right? The two little girls?'

'That's right.'

'We refer to them as the Jacobson murders, the name of the man who was convicted. So tell me how you think we can help your enquiries. Take as long as you wish. I work very flexible hours and I'm not going to rush off home at six o'clock.'

'Thanks. Well, first I need to explain what has happened in our force area.' He provided her with a brief summary of the Ashwell Priory woods murder and the disappearance of Father John Attwood, at this stage refraining from any reference to the real identity of either man. She listened intently, not interrupting his narrative but occasionally jotting notes on a pad.

When Brian had completed his account, she paused and then asked, 'So why does Chief Super Napier link the killing of that man with the Jacobson murders? Has he any evidence to support that?'

'He hasn't officially linked them, Pauline. Both he and I are trying to keep the two enquiries separate but the more we get into our stride, a greater number of linking strands emerge. Let's face it, the timing of the death and the disappearance of the monk, not to mention the venues, are virtually one and the same. Like most crime investigators, I don't believe in coincidences but we do need to examine events very closely.'

'I understand. Now tell me what you know about our Jacobson murders.' She tapped a small package by her side. 'This disc contains a summary of our files and you have my boss's permission to take it if it will be any use. It's a certified copy and your force can keep it. There's also a selection of official photographs on the disc – they might help.'

'Thanks, it'll be most useful. So how much do *you* know about those murders?' he asked.

'Only what I've read in this file. As I said, the murders happened before I joined the force.'

'Can you summarize that file for me? Very briefly?' he asked.

'I'll do my best. The case focuses on a young family called Goddard: Michael aged thirty-one and his wife Geraldine who was twenty-eight. They lived in a mid-terrace house in a street just off Oxford Road in south Manchester. A pleasant area and they owned their house, on a mortgage. Outwardly an ordinary family. They had two daughters, twins aged six. Sophie and

Eleanor. Michael worked as a camera salesman selling to retailers and Geraldine did
part-time work in one of the local shops – a
small general store, a corner shop that sold
everything.'

'A pleasant domestic picture?' commented
Lindsey.

'It was. Outwardly, they presented the false
image of a perfectly normal family, happy
and well balanced. Then tragedy struck.
Geraldine went out one night with her twin
sister, Jenny, to celebrate their birthdays with
a meal and a visit to a club in town. Michael
said he would baby-sit – child-sit is perhaps a
better word – so that the women could have
a good time then get a taxi home. Geraldine
left the house just after seven that evening;
her sister made her own way there.'

'Did the sisters live at the same house?'

'No, Jenny lived about half a mile away.'

'Sorry to interrupt, but go on.'

'About half past nine, Michael decided to
pop out to get a half-dozen pack of cans of
beer from a nearby off licence. It was one of
his regular habits. He expected to be away
for only a few minutes.'

'So he left the girls alone?' He wanted that
point clarified.

'Yes, they were in bed and asleep when he
left the house. He checked before he went
out and locked the door when he left.'

'So for a brief time they were unattended?

Six-year-olds?'

'Right, but it's not as bad as it would appear. They had a very good neighbour, a widower in his early forties, who had a key and would often baby-sit for them, or look after the house if they went away for the weekend. They did that quite regularly, often staying in caravans. Anyway, if either Michael or Geraldine wanted the neighbour to look after the kids temporarily or just to pop his head into the house to see if things were OK, they would ask, and they had a system of rapping on his front window as they left their house. Three loud raps meant a request to look in on the kids. That habit removed the need to knock on the door and disturb the neighbour.'

'A curious practice?'

'Yes, but they often used it and it apparently worked.'

'How did they know he was in?'

'He watched a lot of television in that room. They could hear it and he could hear the raps above the noise. The Goddards and their neighbour had done this for a few years. They told him in advance when they would be leaving and the knocks were confirmation they'd left the house. The neighbour would then pop around to see if the girls were OK. He had a key. He'd stay a while to read them a story if they were awake, and then go home when they were asleep. He would sit all evening if asked but the Goddards didn't like to trouble him too much. They regarded him as an old man – he had a few premature grey hairs and a bald patch.'

'And during those few minutes, somebody went in and killed the girls?'

'Right. It was that man, their neighbour. John Jacobson. He was caught by Michael when he returned from the off licence.'

'Caught?'

'With a carving knife in his hands, both girls dead and blood all over the place. Both had had their throats cut.'

'That's dreadful! So what was Jacobson's story?'

'He told the investigating officer he'd come to check on the girls and had found them dead in bed, with the knife on the bedcovers and blood everywhere. He'd moved the knife and did his best for the girls, then Goddard returned to find him at the bedside, covered in blood. He denied killing them but admitted he'd not disturbed an intruder. Michael, the father, had an alibi – he was in the off licence at that time. And the mother was out with her sister. Both alibis were confirmed.'

'And Jacobson continued to deny the murders?'

'He did. He protested his innocence and the whole affair was very thoroughly investi-

171

gated. Obviously, the father – stepfather to be correct, he was not the girls' natural father – came into the frame as a suspect but apart from an alibi – a partial alibi in reality – the bloodstains on him, and his fingerprints on the murder weapon were explained when he found the girls and wrested the knife from Jacobson. Both men were bloodstained and both sets of fingerprints were on the carving knife. Forensic tests confirmed that.'

'And there's always a strong belief that a father is unlikely to kill his own children. That unsupported belief could tip things in the father's favour.'

'Which is what Goddard said when interviewed. He was distraught at the suggestion he could kill his own wife's offspring. He behaved like their real father. But you and I know tragedies can happen for a variety of reasons.'

'Goddard was thoroughly investigated, was he?'

'As thoroughly as possible. He was a strong suspect, Brian, this file confirms that. He could have killed the children before going out to the off licence. We learned that he was under a lot of pressure at work – he depended heavily on commission as a camera salesman, but sales were going down due to the increased use of mobile phones for taking photographs. He had domestic debts too, and was behind with his mortgage payments.

And we discovered he was not the natural father of those girls – his wife had been unfaithful but because he could not father children he forgave her and accepted the girls as his own. Or so he told everyone.'

'Quite a tangled web! My own police experience has told me there are many apparently devoted fathers who have killed their children. Their motives have been varied – problems at work, loss of status, money worries, mental problems, the wife's behaviour, unfaithfulness, professional insecurity, depression, jealousy or even an ability to control themselves which results in violent outbursts ... there are many cases of fathers losing control, along with motives galore.'

'We are aware of all those, and there was more, Brian. Michael Goddard had a host of troubles and we know he used violence against his wife at times but I've not found any reports of him attacking the children. As a young man he had convictions for assault occasioning actual bodily harm and for carrying offensive weapons – knives, in fact. More importantly, he was involved in the drugs scene – when his salesman's income dwindled, he started dealing in drugs in a small way at first, in and around Manchester. Whilst maintaining the aura of a normal family, he got involved in bigger drug deals despite attempts by other dealers to warn him off, even with death threats. He realized he could beat them at their own game, and became more violent than them. Over the years, he came into the frame for several unsolved murders, all drugs related. Nothing was ever proved. He covered his tracks and silenced witnesses but also moved house regularly to conceal any local notoriety and also took on modest jobs to give him the appearance of a family man. He was a very clever villain.'

'So despite all that known background, he was never charged with those child murders? And John Jacobson was found guilty?'

'He was interviewed, that was a foregone conclusion but Goddard's alibi was a key factor, Brian.'

'Tell me about it.'

'Before going to the off licence he was alone in the house with the girls. His alibi was his visit to the off licence which was confirmed and, of course, the fact that he had caught Jacobson in the girls' room with a knife in his hands and covered in blood. He took the knife from Jacobson and got blood on his own hands by doing so, that was his story. Goddard's fingerprints were found on the carving knife and he had blood all over his clothing and hands. It was their blood, forensic evidence proved that. Goddard's account was accepted.

'The girls had died a bloody death; the sheets and Jacobson's hands and clothes were covered with their blood. He even had the knife in his hand as Goddard walked in. Caught bang to rights, as they say.'

'That seems very conclusive but it does give rise to a need for closer questioning of Goddard. Do we know anything else against Jacobson?'

'Not a lot. He was a widower with no family; his wife had died some years earlier and he had worked in the building trade. He had retired early, selling his business but then earning extra by doing odd jobs, house repairs mainly. He had no convictions and was widely regarded as a very decent man. Defence counsel tried to convince the jury that he was innocent but they heard a story of him sitting on the bed with the girls on an earlier occasion. When this was followed by the father's evidence that he had caught Jacobson in the girls' bedroom, knife in hand and blood all over, it was enough to convince the jury. When he was convicted, people in the public gallery applauded. He was sentenced to life imprisonment with a recommendation he should never be released so long as he was a danger to children. His defence counsel helped him to sell his house on the grounds he would probably never be released. Despite all the evidence against him, coupled with the court decision, Jacobson continued to protest his innocence but all in vain. The problem was he could not prove his innocence. The evidence was overwhelming.'

'So what happened to the Goddards?'

'They sold the house and moved away. The girls' natural father was a drug dealer too but he was killed in a traffic accident. Informers said Goddard was responsible for setting it up – there was intense enmity between them – but nothing was proved. Goddard was questioned but never charged. After the girls' murder, they moved around very frequently, always using a legitimate business and change of address to conceal their drugs activities. We lost track of them; they never returned to the Manchester area.'

'You must have had enquiries about them? From other police forces?'

'For a while, yes, but their links with Lancashire faded away. Recently we learned that Michael had set up a business somewhere in Yorkshire making shockproof and waterproof cases for mobile phones and vulnerable things like pocket calculators, cameras and even spectacles. Another cover for his drug dealing. Word has it that he's a successful businessman in the York area, and his wife is still with him, but they have no family. I'm sure his wife never knew he had killed the children. Jacobson carried all the blame. If the Goddards are around and involved in their usual business, they'll be operating under false names, they always do.'

'Still violent, is he? Is that something you know?'

'Yes, we are fed snippets from time to time. As I've said, it's known he's a violent but charming rogue, Brian, the worst of the worst. And he can silence witnesses. On top of that, he's become extremely rich.'

'If he's in the York area, we can check him out. I wonder if he's come across Jacobson, who's also living in Yorkshire? You know he's out of prison, do you?' Brian put to Pauline.

'Our last information was that Jacobson would never admit to the crime, so he would never be granted parole. You say he's out now?'

'Yes, on licence. Much to everyone's surprise, he admitted his guilt and was granted parole. He has been out for ten years or so, living under an assumed name in our force area, which is why I'm aware of this. I am sure there will be a record somewhere in your offices, perhaps in a top secret file.'

'We should have been informed. He'll be under strict supervision, surely?'

'Naturally. But I have to say this – he is now known as Father John Attwood and is a monk at Maddleskirk Abbey deep in the moors near Aidensfield. He disappeared on Saturday shortly before a murdered man was found near the monastery. There's a search going on for him right now.'

'That sounds ominous! Someone's not

been too careful with their supervision. Who's the dead man?'

'We're not sure. Very few people know about Father Attwood's past and it is not for public consumption. From what we are told, it seems he admitted the crimes simply to get out of prison so that he could set about proving his innocence.'

'You say he has disappeared? Was that voluntarily?'

'He might have been tricked into leaving the monastery.'

'That sounds nasty. Have you met him?'

'No, I haven't, but we are investigating the murder of an unknown man in the woods near the abbey. He was killed with a stiletto wound, the trademark of a drugs baron. The circumstances are puzzling but my boss, Detective Chief Superintendent Napier, wants to know more about the crime for which he was convicted, hence my visit here. He reckons it's relevant.'

'He's not suggesting this force manipulated the conviction of an innocent man, is he?'

'I'm sure he would suggest no such thing, Pauline. The evidence was enough to convince the jury. That's pretty final. The case appears to have been conducted according to the rules.'

'It was, but I have to admit there were doubts about that conviction. Before you arrived, I spoke to officers who remember the case and out of the three I spoke to, two expressed doubts. They felt Jacobson had been set up for the murder and that the crime was the work of the girls' stepfather. The possibility was investigated discreetly but evidence of Jacobson's guilt was too strong – enough to convince the senior investigating officer and a jury.'

'Do you think your chief constable would sanction a cold-case review? It would help us to deal with the present murder.'

'Your boss needs to speak to my chief,' suggested Pauline. 'But I would add my support – after all, I've read a summary and must say that gave me doubts about the safety of Jacobson's conviction. There are some points of evidence that seem not to have been checked, overlooked by both the investigating team and Jacobson's defence counsel.'

'And it would be necessary to re-examine the forensic evidence.'

'That can be done,' she said. 'But I am powerless to help – a cold-case review is a matter for our chiefs, yours and mine. And don't forget, Brian, cold-case reviews can take a long time.'

'I'll bear that in mind. Thanks for taking the time to talk to me like this and thanks for producing this disc, it will be most useful. Now I'll let you go home.'

'You'll keep me informed?'

'Of course.'

Chapter 12

'You were late back, Brian!' commented Detective Chief Superintendent Napier the next morning, Tuesday.

'There was a lot to investigate, boss.'

'So what's your verdict? Was your trip useful?'

'Yes. Very.' He provided a short resumé, adding, 'It takes us a step or two forward. Of major importance is confirmation that the stepfather of the Jacobson victims, Michael Goddard, has moved from Manchester. No one is sure where he's gone, he has disappeared with his wife, and they're thought to be living in the York area under assumed names. He is a known killer, taking out those who get in his way, but he appears to be a highly successful businessman. A cover story. One of his enterprises is making safety covers for mobile phones, calculators and so on, but the Criminal Intelligence Bureau along with Manchester CID believe his real wealth comes from drug dealing under the guise of various forms of manufacturing. He shouldn't be hard to trace if we can find the right people but this inquiry has shifted firmly into our lap. We should realize that if

Goddard is currently operating on our patch, he might have seen Father John somewhere and recognized him despite a few years of ageing and John's new identity.'

'If that happened, what would be Goddard's reaction? Any ideas?'

'Shock at first, then disbelief at seeing John free from prison, especially if he had framed him. Goddard would want to make sure his own future wasn't at risk. If he saw John out of prison and moving around the countryside quite freely, Goddard would do his utmost to eliminate him to safeguard himself. He would take whatever action necessary to stop him – such as death or framing him for another murder?'

'That's how I read the situation, Brian, but I can assure you that John is safe for the time being. I'll explain eventually. Now we must concentrate on Goddard, who is a dangerous and slippery customer. We must persuade him to come into the open – where we shall be waiting. The only way to nail him is to trap him, Brian.'

'He'll smell a rat, surely? Whatever tactics we use.'

'Not if we're cunning! There are matters you don't know yet but Father John is the bait. He has something that will be bothering Goddard. Father John has a file stored in a secret place – it contains evidence that could convict Goddard. We've made sure he knows about it and he intends to destroy it. Even if he kills John, he can never be safe with that file lying around. And there's another thing, Brian. The dead man in the wood, the undercover police officer, was watching Father John, not trying to catch him committing a breach of his licence, but protecting him. And see what happened to him!'

'Goddard got rid of him?'

'Who else? Who else would have a motive? Goddard is quite capable of killing an undercover agent to protect his own back.'

'That woman we're trying to identify? The one in the confessional? Could she be Goddard's wife, mother of the dead girls? Conspiring with him to eliminate Father John?'

'Mrs Goddard is involved with all his projects, legal or not. She might even be the brains behind some of her husband's endeavours. We can't ignore her, Brian.'

'I find it difficult to understand why she doesn't suspect that her husband killed her girls?'

'That's Goddard for you. It shows something of his treachery and cunning. I'm sure she has no idea.'

'So will she be with Goddard now, somewhere on our patch?'

'Almost certainly. In fact, Nick Rhea discovered a witness who saw a woman with Radcliffe near St Valentine's Well. I showed the witness – Claude Jeremiah Greengrass –

a still from the CCTV coverage of the south transept but he couldn't be sure it was the same woman. All he said was that it might be her, not that it was. That's not good enough for us, Brian, we need to be sure – but in spite of that, it's a lead. So how much detail of the Jacobson murders is available to us?'

'I've got the entire file on disc including photos and Detective Chief Inspector Hammond has promised all the assistance she can give.'

'We need our best officers to concentrate on finding Goddard without approaching him or alerting him. We must establish where he is and what he's up to.'

'Do we need to consider his wife's sister?' asked Brian.

'Do you think she's involved?'

'It's possible. On the night of the murders Geraldine Goddard was having a night out with her sister, celebrating their birthdays. In the plural. Twins in fact. She could know more than anyone has realized. That woman that Greengrass noticed talking to the murdered detective could have been her.'

'Are you saying the sister is working *against* the Goddards? That's dangerous but not impossible. Certainly the woman who met Father John outside Scarborough Beach Hospital looked very similar to the one who used the confessional. Maybe the sister is working for the security service, Brian? Something undercover. Police even!'

'We have no information about the sister except her first name is Jenny.'

'There are a lot of tangled strands to unravel, Brian. You're the man to sort it all out so I'll release you from supervising the murder room – DS Salkeld can continue. It's good experience for her. So there we are, your job is to catch Goddard.'

'I'll be pleased to tackle it.'

'Good. Select two good detectives from those working here. They'll be your specialist team. Spread the news among the criminal underworld that you're trying to trace the Goddards under whatever name they're operating. Get the local smalltime criminals stirred up while you're at it. Get them worried … they'll soon filter information down to your team just to get you off their backs. Leave Father John to us.'

'Right, boss.'

'Now let's go. I'm going to brief the teams.'

Quite deliberately, Napier had withheld some information from DI Lindsey and he had also decided not yet to release the true identity of the murder victim to his other officers. But he would tell them about Father John Attwood. He believed his criminal record would encourage the teams to respond with more enthusiasm if they believed they were hunting a convicted child killer.

Napier therefore instructed his team leaders to inform their detectives that finding Father Attwood dead or alive must be given the highest priority. He stressed the monk was in possession of information that was important to the current investigation. 'You must find him; we need to hear his full story.'

Napier followed with a brief account of Attwood/Jacobson's conviction for two child murders whilst reinforcing earlier orders that this information was not for public consumption and, at this stage, definitely not for the media. He explained that DI Lindsey and his team were concentrating on a branch of the investigation in the York area, but told them that the information about the monk's former life was known only to the people in the murder room – and that included the shocked monkstables.

He exhorted them to continue their search for witnesses, particularly the woman who had been seen by Claude Jeremiah Greengrass, and he stressed they should not abandon efforts to trace people who had attended confession on Saturday. It was vital they traced the woman with the umbrella whose grainy photograph was now posted on a board in the murder room. Napier reminded them that much of the interviewing and searching would be repetitive or even boring, but added, 'The answer is out there somewhere and it's our job to find it. Now, Nick Rhea, can you hang on a moment, I'd like a word?'

'Sure.'

As everyone set about their actions and updated their own personal files, Napier signalled to Nick. 'My office, Nick. Now.'

When they were settled in the cramped accommodation, Napier said, 'I have an unpleasant job to do, Nick, and I'd appreciate your presence whilst I'm doing it.'

'Why me?'

'Because you have one foot in our police camp and another one in this abbey and its complement of monks. I just need you to be present, to make sure I don't do something that's markedly off limits.'

'What on earth are we going to do?'

'Search Father John's room.'

'That is not a very pleasant thing to do, is it?' Nick expressed his own views. 'It's an invasion of a monk's privacy.'

'That's why I want you with me. You know about these things, the niceties in such cases.'

'I wouldn't bank on that, Mr Napier, but of course I'll help. Wouldn't the prior be a better companion?'

'I thought about him but he's too close to the men under his wing. You're independent. I know it's not a pleasant job but for the progress of this investigation, it must be done. I've got the abbot's reluctant approval.'

'What will you be looking for?'

'I've no idea until I find it. Hopefully, it will be something that guides us to John's present whereabouts; a diary entry perhaps, a letter. But I suspect he has something else that's very valuable, and not merely to us. As this man spent a long time in prison and several years on release wanting to prove his innocence, he must have gathered information that he could present to the police or to an appeal court. Even to the press. We need to find whatever he's collected and examine it – and safeguard it from Goddard. Where do I get his key?'

'The prior will have a spare. I expect Father John will have his own with him.'

'If he's being held against his will, his key might have been found and the villains might come looking for that file, to destroy it. Can anyone gain entry to his room? How secure is the monastic area of the abbey?'

Nick explained about the coded entry door, telling Napier there were no names on any of the monks' rooms whilst security devices were in place to protect the private areas used only by monks, such as their library and lounge.

'And,' said Nick, smiling, 'there's a large

187

notice saying "No Admittance to Women".'

'That won't stop a determined wrong-doer, or a determined woman!'

'From my previous experience, I believe each monk is responsible for the security of his own cell. All doors are self-locking and the windows overlook the cloister and court-yard, both of which are secure.'

'Fair enough. Let's get the key. If the abbey authorities try to prevent me, I shall obtain a search warrant on the grounds we're looking for evidence of murder. And that means we could smash the door down.'

'That would make us popular!'

'Tough. But I don't want to do that unless there's no alternative. Come along, lead me to Friar Tuck.'

Napier explained his requirements when they found the prior in the Postgate Room but despite the abbot's consent, the prior shrank from the idea of anyone searching a brother monk's private quarters. Napier, however, was not going to be diverted. After he had explained and then expounded his actions if he was refused access, Father Prior capitulated.

'I'll get a key. Meet me at the entrance to the monastery.'

Nick led the way through the network of corridors until they arrived at the entrance to a long wide corridor with a succession of identical doors along its route. There were also staircases leading to two higher floors. Here they halted to wait.

'I always thought the term monastery means the entire place,' admitted Napier. 'Now I realize it's only that part where the monks live and sleep, have their own rooms, library, refectory, library and lounge.'

'Right.' Nick nodded. 'The abbey is the all-embracing name for the entire complex. The abbey church is self-explanatory. There are other places such as the theatre, sports complex, infirmary, reception, visitor centre, transport department, estate manager, farm and so forth – all making up one huge establishment called an abbey. It's more than just a ruined church! In this particular case, there are additional buildings. I mean, the college with all its classrooms, lecture theatres, accommodation blocks, sports areas and so on – but all part of this abbey.'

'In this job you learn something new every day. Ah, here comes our man with the key. You'd better come with us, Friar Tuck.'

The accommodation was made up of a single bedroom with en suite bathroom, a lounge and a study. It was meticulously tidy but somewhat sparsely furnished, the walls being covered in emulsion in a neutral shade. There were no ornaments or wall pictures, except for those associated with religion. There was a small desk supporting a computer and printer. Around the room

189

were a bookcase, a wardrobe and a chest of drawers that also served as a dressing table with a small rug under its chair. A small wooden crucifix stood on the dressing table.

'This won't take us long,' muttered Napier and for a few minutes he stood in the centre of the room and gazed around, absorbing all the detail. 'Here, we'd better wear these,' and like a magician he produced from his pocket some pairs of Latex gloves used by SOCO for such searches. Then he addressed Nick.

'Can you search the wardrobe, open any suitcases and check the pockets of every garment in there. If you ask what you'll be looking for, I have no idea – you'll know if you come across something that might be relevant. I'll have a look around his desk, checking any files or papers, and I'll go through that chest of drawers. We might also have to dig into the stuff stored in his computer but that means taking it away.'

'We've the skills to do that,' Prior Tuck reminded him.

Their searches were brief simply because they produced nothing of interest. They replaced everything as they had found it in the knowledge that Father John, when he returned, would never know his room had been searched.

He had very few personal possessions whilst the bathroom contained his tooth-brush, razor and washing materials.

'He didn't expect to be away for long – he didn't take his overnight stuff,' commented Napier, acting as if he was not aware of the background to these actions. 'This hasn't produced anything of interest and there's no loft entrance here.'

'How about under the bed?' suggested Nick, noticing the covers reached almost to the floor. He bent down, lifted up one side of the cover and found a large cardboard storage box of the kind used to store dead-section files. He gave it a push and it slid easily on the polished floor, emerging at the far side of the bed.

'This could be interesting,' breathed Napier. 'Thanks, Nick. For a moment I'd forgotten my elementary tuition in searching. Always look under the bed! So what have we here?'

The top was not sealed so it was easy to open it and see neatly stored files. Napier eased one out; it held dated newspaper cuttings of the Jacobson trial. Others contained more cuttings, each file representing a day at the trial, with evidence in detail. And there were print-outs from his computer with several hand-written notes.

One said, 'It was raining whilst Michael was at the off licence but he wasn't wet when he returned...' There was no explanation for that comment. Another said, 'I remember being in the Goddards' house and hearing the ground floor toilet being flushed … I thought I was alone but realized I wasn't. And I heard the loft floor creaking above, as if someone was up there…'

'This could be very important.' Napier's faced showed a glow of pleasure. 'He's gone through the newspaper reports and picked holes in the evidence that was presented in court, then added his own observations. Friar Tuck, we're seizing this box of papers as evidence.'

'I understand,' said the prior softly.

Napier continued, 'I'll need someone to take this computer to the murder room. We can carry this box of papers between us. I think Detective Inspector Lindsey will have to make time to go through this lot in detail…'

They left with the box and locked the door, Napier taking the key.

Chapter 13

Detective Chief Superintendent Napier managed to make space on a shelf in his cramped office and they pushed the large box of papers into it.

'I'll get Brian to go through this – it needs to be done very soon.'

'Maybe I could help?' offered Nick.

'That might be a good idea; you're familiar with the case. What are you doing next?'

'I've no commitments other than dealing with the inputs that arrive in the Postgate Room. The monkstables are very active with local enquiries, they seem to relish interviewing people and taking statements.'

There was a knock on Napier's partially open door and Detective Sergeant Salkeld appeared.

'Yes, Sarge, what can I do for you?' Napier asked.

'Father John's computer has been delivered. Our boffins will get busy on it straightaway but we've had a breakthrough of sorts, Mr Napier. I thought you should know.'

'Too right I should know! What's happened?'

'The woman who met Father Attwood outside Scarborough's Beach Hospital. We've got her car reg. She'd parked outside the hospital grounds in the shadows of a row of trees. The parking area belongs to the hospital and they've a CCTV camera there. It shows her and Father John getting into the car and moving off towards the town. She was driving. There was no one else in the car. We've checked the registration number – it's a hire car.'

'That means we can trace her through the

hire company.'

'We're on to that right now. It's a local firm with an office in Scarborough.'

'Good, let me know the result the minute it's available. And another thing, circulate that car reg all around Scarborough and district, let every copper on duty know about it. We need sightings, details of occupants, direction of travel, fuel being bought, stopping places with times being noted. Anything and everything. Check local traffic control cameras too, sometimes they can produce results. Somebody must have seen that car.'

'I'll make sure the town patrols get busy!'

As Detective Sergeant Salkeld returned to her duty of managing the murder room, Napier felt proud of his continuing deception as he summoned a detective constable and said, 'DC Simpson, you're a strong young man, give Mr Rhea a hand with that box, can you? It's heading for the Postgate Room.'

'Sir.' And the deed was done.

The Postgate Room was almost deserted when Nick arrived, save for Father Will, who was checking some papers he'd not read due to his duties in the cop shop. As the monkstables had gone off to fulfil their allocated tasks, he'd taken this opportunity to update himself. He looked up and smiled as Nick and the detective bore the heavy box into the room and placed it on the central table. The detective departed with Nick's thanks as Father Will said, 'That's Father John's box of papers, isn't it?'

'You recognize it?'

'Yes, I do. I often helped him with his filing. That box contains files from his murder trial. It's a very comprehensive account of the whole sorry affair with his own observations.'

'He must have trusted you. Did you get the impression he was not guilty?'

'Certainly! There's stuff in that box that I'm sure could prove his innocence. He's not a bitter man, Nick, just very disappointed with British justice.'

'Then we need to help him all we can. How did you come into contact with him?' asked Nick.

'Just a chat in the grounds one day, not long after he joined the monastery. He didn't know anyone, didn't have friends here, and quite often we found ourselves walking together across the valley in our private times. Eventually, as the days passed, we grew more friendly and he discussed his past with me. I was shocked to say the least but he demanded my silence until he decided to make more people aware of events that led to his trial. Whenever I had the time, I helped him to sort through all these papers and notes. I helped him to record all the facts and information. I showed him how to use a computer to make things easier, even to downloading newspaper reports from old newspapers, then checking and indexing their contents.'

'Was the computer record downloaded into this box, or is it still in his computer's memory?'

'Both, he's a belt-and-braces man, Nick. Even though we managed to assemble the information on his computer, he insisted on paper records as well. Maybe it is easier to read them on paper, as he suggests. But everything's available. I hope it helps to prove his innocence.'

'Before that happens, Father Will, we'll need him to explain things in person. He was there, remember. We weren't.'

'I just hope we find him before anyone else does. I'll be pleased to help. I'm familiar with that material and I know his system. It's a bit quiet in the cop shop at the moment – everything seems to be happening elsewhere!'

'I'll talk to Mr Napier,' said Nick. He picked up the phone and dialled Napier's number, then explained the situation.

'That's brilliant. Get Father Will to help as much he can. I know he'll be discreet. Can you both work out of sight in the cop shop? It's not exactly crowded in there, is it? Lock the door and put a closed sign up! Don't let all and sundry read Father John's files.' Napier rang off.

Nick and Father Will returned to the cop

shop to scrutinize Father John's records.

Meanwhile, Detective Inspector Lindsey and his officers were trying to locate people called Goddard who lived in the York area, or in York city itself. They knew that would not be the name they'd be using now but they had to start somewhere. The first point of reference was the local telephone directory but there were more than two dozen references, three listed as M. Goddard and one as G. Goddard. Lindsey rang them all. Two of the M. Goddards were at home but none was Michael. G. Goddard was a woman but her name was Grace. None of them knew of a family Goddard who had moved from Manchester.

As his officers worked, DI Lindsey decided to seek assistance from the BT Criminal Investigation Branch. His office and the BTCIB were in regular contact about crimes and offences that impacted upon both organizations.

He rang a dedicated number. A voice answered: 'Temperley

'Good morning, Joe, it's Lindsey, North Yorkshire CID.'

'Hi there, Brian. How's things in that great wilderness called Yorkshire?'

'Busy as ever. Criminal investigation is endless! Sorry to trouble you but we've a tricky murder investigation ongoing at the moment. I could do with your expertise.'

'Always willing to help the constabulary. What can I do?'

Without releasing too much sensitive detail, Brian explained he was trying to trace some Goddards who had moved to the York area from Manchester, probably to establish a small family business. He wanted to know if such people had recruited the assistance of BT for their telephone, internet or any other service. Brian explained that he could not be certain about the date of their arrival but it could have been several years ago.

'Things are changing all the time, Brian. Our technology has moved on and our older files are obsolete. Mind, we have kept some which we can still access. I'll run all your local Goddards through the computer which will highlight the dates when their BT phones or any other devices and services were connected. We can take things from there. Give me a couple of hours then I'll email you with the result.'

'That's a good start, thanks.'

'You realize, don't you, that an ever-increasing number of people and businesses are no longer using our network? For one thing, they're turning to mobile phones, and that includes businesses, not just individuals. There are other servers so you've a lot of digging to do if you're to find those people, especially if their business is not under the proprietor's name. Most are probably under the company name or names.'

'I realize that. If it's any help, I've been told my target has ventured into the world of waterproof and shockproof cases for portable items, cases that would bear an elephant standing on them in ten fathoms. Indestructible by all accounts. Good stuff!'

'You say he was called Goddard from Manchester? Our technical branch does get bags of publicity material, spam most of it, but now and again something more interesting pops up. He might have tried to interest us in his products. Having said that, individuals are getting more difficult to trace. Everyone moves around a lot these days and there are people and businesses with more than one mobile phone and no landline, some operating from different venues, some overseas. Anyway, leave it with me. I'll see what our computer wizardry can turn up. We're not known as the Investigation Branch for nothing!'

'Thanks, and if I can return the favour, just let me know.'

'There's no doubt I will sooner or later. See you, Brian.' And he ended the call.

Next, Brian Lindsey made a similar call to a friend and colleague who worked from York Police Station as a detective inspector. He was DI Malcolm Ainsley. After the usual introductory chat, he said, 'We've received circulars about your murder inquiry, Brian. Sounds like a tricky one.'

'It is,' Brian stressed, adding a brief summary. 'We've managed to keep it under wraps without any media interest. That's one of the benefits of working in a massive rural area but in any case, our local reporters are very co-operative when the need is there. One line of inquiry is that drugs might be involved. We need to trace the Goddards without them being aware of our interest.'

'Mum's the word, as they say,' promised Ainsley. 'My team knows what's going on, nothing much gets past them. We have some fairly new business and industrial parks on the outskirts and in any case I'll run a check through our local intelligence files to check the drugs situation. I'll call you if we turn up anything.'

And so Detective Inspector Lindsey, knowing these activities would soon reach the ears of the local criminal fraternity, worked steadily through all his reliable contacts as he resorted to the old-fashioned way of crime investigation – you told as many detectives and police officers as possible and so recruited dozens of pairs of extra ears and eyes to help in your work. In so doing, pressure was exerted on the criminal fraternity. He had no doubt that the newspapers, local radio and television stations could also help but at this juncture Napier would not agree to that. He had not informed PA or any other press agency and there was no guarantee how they would treat the facts if they were alerted. Indeed, widespread publicity might cause the targets to run for cover. Napier did not want that – he wanted to flush out the villains so that they scuttled about like startled rabbits, to be led eventually into his trap.

DI Lindsey knew that if the Goddards *had* moved to live and work in or near York, someone must have encountered them or done business with them; in short, they would be traced. In view of their past notoriety, some of those encounters could have been with police officers.

As the well-oiled machinery of the wider investigation got into its stride, masses of information flowed into the murder room from officers busy with external enquiries. Working in the Postgate Room, Nick was also aware of the valuable input from the monkstables, whose area of operations had now spread to local villages. As the wealth of information steadily accumulated without producing a much-needed breakthrough, Nick decided to get some fresh air.

He needed some thinking time and so, in the bright sunshine of that September day, he excused himself temporarily from Father Will and the box of papers. Will said he would take a break too – too much close concentration gave him headaches. As

Father Will relaxed by standing near the cop shop counter to deal with any customers, Nick went outside.

For ten minutes or so he walked around the grounds, because he found one matter increasingly worrying. That concern had been intensified by his brief scrutiny of Father John's papers. There was no doubt that Father John had been cleverly framed for the Jacobson murders, and consequently strong contradictory evidence was needed. Father John's handwritten notes had been compiled long after the trail. Too late for the jury to consider them.

John's notes were, in reality, a gathering of very small matters that had escaped the notice of his defence counsel. Those flaws seemed trivial against the might of the accusation levelled against him and the cross he'd had to bear. However, one area for examination was the precise timing and locations of John's movements in the house when Michael Goddard swore he was at the off licence. There was the matter of rain falling heavily but when Michael returned from the off licence his hair and clothing were dry. John claimed he had heard noises in the house, such as movements in the loft and the ground floor toilet being flushed, when the house was supposedly empty apart from the girls who were upstairs in bed. But how could he prove that? And what was the design of the house? It could be a factor.

According to Father John, Michael Goddard had been to the off licence – that was not in doubt – but the file indicated that the counter assistant had thought it was some time earlier than Michael had stated. She couldn't be sure but the time had never been analyzed.

Michael was a regular customer whose visiting times varied considerably. Michael had insisted his timing was accurate – after all, he had used their own special message system by tapping on the window to signal John's presence was needed as a child-sitter. John would know what time those tapping noises had occurred. But that was not all that troubled Nick.

As he pondered the tumble of events, he felt that not enough was currently being done to search for the missing monk. For one thing, there was no publicity. That could be done without any reference to the murder inquiry – they would be portrayed as quite separate incidents. In fact, a monk not returning from hospital was not really newsworthy, and at this stage the murder could be billed as nothing more than an unidentified body found in woodland. With no police cars and ambulances with flashing blue lights, public interest would not yet have been ignited.

It could be said that on Saturday night no

one had found cause for alarm, even though Father John had not returned to the monastery. The truth was that no one had expected him back until later that night, especially if he used the public bus service, and the campus was sufficiently large for such a return, however late, to go unnoticed. Indeed, it was very likely he may have been required to remain overnight, the hospital providing the necessary attire and toilet requisites. Sunday had passed without any cause for alarm and it was not until yesterday, Monday, that any kind of concern had surfaced. So had anyone rung the hospital to check these events? Nick had an uneasy feeling that his colleagues in the murder room were not exerting sufficient effort to find the missing monk. Did they simply believe he had run off with a woman after a rendezvous at the hospital gates, and then vanished in a hired car? Hardly matters for the police!

But none of this musing provided any clue to Father John's whereabouts or indeed his present state of health. Even more important, was he in any danger? If so, from whom? The Goddards? Were they closing in on him? Indeed, had they found him and removed him from circulation by their own simple deception?

Undecided about his response to this, Nick wondered whether he could or should seek to energize what he regarded as a very low-key search. He could do that by reverting to his earlier role as a police press officer and contacting the local media. Getting the press involved would put the proverbial cat among the pigeons, but it would result in a lot of people looking for Father John, whatever he had done or not done.

Nick knew that if he surreptitiously approached the press it would anger Detective Chief Superintendent Napier. So was there a reason for Napier's low-key approach? Perhaps he had very deep reasons for *not* seeking to involve the media?

Was Napier deliberately concealing information? If so, why?

Nick began to ponder the trustworthiness of Detective Chief Superintendent 'Nabber' Napier.

Chapter 14

Unsettled by his thoughts, Nick diverted from his route back to the cop shop and headed for the murder room. It was as busy as ever with the noise of people talking on telephones above the clatter of keyboards and printers, and there was the persistent buzz of a very active operations centre.

Detective Sergeant Salkeld noticed his arrival and called, 'Over here, Nick.' She was sitting at the desk normally occupied by DI Lindsey. 'Can I help?'

'I've been walking in the grounds to get some fresh air and marshal my thoughts. I must admit I'm concerned about the lack of effort in the search for Father John. I wondered whether the media could help by alerting the public?'

'The boss has ordered us not to talk to the press, Nick. If they do call us, he will deal with them. And that's final.'

'Well, I can't argue with that even if I don't understand the reasons, so have there been any developments?'

'We've traced the hire car at Scarborough but it wasn't used by our targets. It was another man and woman, quite legitimate. However, Nick, we have traced a taxi that was used by Father John and his lady companion. Her description matched our target and her companion was a clergyman with a dog collar. They were picked up at the hospital and dropped near the railway station, and from that point onwards we've had no reports. They've disappeared into thin air. The taxi driver thought they'd gone to catch a train but he didn't ask any questions. The woman paid the taxi fare, by the way.'

'Deliberately evasive, do you think?'

'It does smack of a deliberate ploy to lose

anyone who might be showing too much interest!'

'But why would anyone go to all this trouble to spirit him away? There's always an element of risk in this kind of thing.'

'We're not sure why such an operation was necessary, Nick, but it raises another question. Was it masterminded by Father John himself? Remember the hospital has no record of him arriving or even being called in to discuss his condition. There are lots of loopholes, a lot of unanswered questions and much to consider.'

'Is Father John being strongly linked to the murder victim? As a suspect, I mean?'

'That can't be avoided, can it? We can't avoid the fact that there is a connection so it's vital we find him, if only to eliminate him from suspicion.'

'I can understand the team thinking along those lines, so is there any further progress with the murder inquiry? And I must say I think it is also very low key...'

'There are reasons, Nick.' Her voice suggested she was quietly warning him not to rush things, not to push his luck. 'Don't try to organize things. I will say, though, that I'm allowed to tell you that the murder victim was a serving police officer and his parent force – the London Met – has been informed. They confirmed his home address and we've notified his relatives but the Met has not revealed what he was doing in this locality. All they would say is that he was on duty and engaged on a covert mission generated by important criminal intelligence that had emanated from the Crime Intelligence Bureau. Mr Napier has not informed the media yet and we've restricted news of the murder by saying it appears to be the sudden death of a visitor, as yet unidentified. The press was happy with that – for the time being.'

'A police officer, you say? Murdered? This mystery gets deeper and deeper and definitely more complex and unnerving.'

'Now you know why Napier doesn't want to involve the press!'

'I'm pleased you've told me. I was going to suggest a news conference to create public interest if we're to find Father John.'

'No chance! Just give us time, Nick. Mr Napier is in charge, remember, and he does know what he is doing. Our activities must be kept as low key as possible for a while longer. I can tell you, though, that the press is aware that something's going on. We've had a call from a local freelance.'

'So what did you tell him?'

'Just what I've told you. Mr Napier said we were investigating the sudden death of an unknown man whose body was found in woodland. For a quote, he said, "At the moment, his identity is unknown and we are trying to establish his personal background. We do not suspect foul play but all the circumstances are being thoroughly investigated."'

'A good noncommittal quote!'

'It is. Even I don't know the whole story and I'm supposed to be running the murder room – but it's easy to do as I'm told!'

'Even with some kind of undercover work going on, we mustn't dispense with the need to use our initiative! OK, I get the message. I'll get back to Father John's box of papers.'

'That's very important to this inquiry, Nick – you might turn up something!'

Now feeling slightly isolated on the periphery of the inquiry, Nick left the murder room with a disturbing feeling that he was involved in something he failed to understand. He returned to Father Will.

He found the bespectacled monk busy in the back room of the cop shop, with neatly arranged piles of paper on the floor around the small desk he was using.

There were some large clear plastic envelopes containing more papers and Nick realized they were computer printouts. Settling on the chair beside the desk, Nick explained the most recent developments in the murder room, stressing the unexplained need for secrecy. Then asked, 'Anything interesting here?'

'I'm beginning to see daylight through this rather heavy fog,' said Father Will. 'We can ignore most of those old newspaper cuttings. They report the arrest of John Jacobson as he was then known, and provide a fairly comprehensive record of the trial that followed. That's all public knowledge.'

'The case attracted massive media coverage, if my memory is correct.'

'The media went ballistic because the case involved two little girls and a friendly "uncle" who lived nearby. Not their real uncle, I hasten to add.'

'Always a hot potato, Father Will.'

'You don't have to remind me – the monastic brethren went through hell at that time too. Everyone thought all monks and priests spent their time assaulting children. The actions of a rotten few caused intense problems for many.'

'I'd left the force at that stage and John hadn't become a monk but I could see how public perception of the truth was destroyed by ill-informed public knowledge. Gossip, in other words. It happens all the time. Anyway, that's all in the past. We've got to concentrate on the matter in mind. What can you tell me?'

'One matter that has emerged is that we know what happened in the girls' home that night, even if it all occurred within a very few minutes.'

'Surely that formed part of John's defence?'

'No, it didn't. That's the problem. These findings were never given in his defence; they were not revealed until later. I can save you a lot of time if I condense them into a few words.'

'So this box of files is his real claim to innocence? Is that right?'

'Yes. We're good friends, Nick. In recent months, he has opened his thoughts and it was me who suggested he write it all down, every tiny thing he could recall. Believe me, Nick, these papers could be dynamite if the press – or anyone else – got hold of them.'

'What do you mean by that?'

'John is innocent which means someone else killed those children. That is a very basic fact, and he knows who is guilty. His claim centres on three houses – John's home was one of them and the other was next door, the house where the girls lived. The third was the off licence. The houses were part of a long terrace. Father John – who worked in the building trade – has produced some sketches which are among these papers.'

'Accurate, are they?'

'As accurate as possible. The trouble is we can't examine any of those houses because they were demolished along with the entire terrace a few years ago to make way for a new road. I think you should examine these papers, Nick, to get a police overview. You might want to take them somewhere quiet.'

'I'll be happy in here, Father Will. You can look after the shop while I examine them, then you'll be here if I want to ask any questions.'

'You need to go through these piles here,' and he indicated those he had separated from the bulk of the material. 'They're John's own work. His sketches and comments. They're important. If you take note of times and places quoted in the official statements, these will convince you that John could not have committed those murders.'

'Wonderful! There's one other thing, Father Will. There seems to be very little concern about Father John's absence. After what you've told me, he's clearly at great risk. Do you know where he is?'

'To answer that specific question, the answer is no.'

'I sense you know something you're not revealing?'

'John spoke to me in confidence, Nick, as a friend. Before he went to the hospital, so can we take this one step at a time, Nick. Please.'

'You realize that his continuing absence is feeding a strong suspicion that he killed the man in the wood, and that he's now on the run? His previous record adds to that! We can't ignore his background even if it is untrue. It will be dynamite if the media find out, especially if they smell a cover-up.'

'I'm aware of that, Nick, but let's leave things as they are right now. Have a look at those papers then we'll talk again.'

Father Will left Nick alone whilst he went to staff the counter of the cop shop. In the limited space of the back room, a somewhat worried Nick set to work.

Chapter 15

'When will I be allowed to leave?' Father John asked Sue.

'When it's safe,' she replied. 'And it's not safe at the moment, please believe me, Father John. I'm doing this for your own good.'

'How can I believe that? I was told to contact you and here I am, a prisoner, I'm locked in. And I know you have a gun.'

'Which means others are locked out and I can protect you. That's my job. You must believe me, Father, no one knows you're here.'

'Where am I? I couldn't follow where you were taking me, all those taxis and the railway station, in and out of shops. I can't attract attention, can I? We're in some sort of high building...'

'It's a fourth-floor flat,' she said. 'A safe house. We use it quite a lot. It's not very salubrious but it is quite anonymous and very handy for the beach and shops if you're here for any length of time...'

'Well, my windows look onto a brick wall and I'm staring all day into a yard. So what am I doing here? I thought I was going to hospital.'

'You're acting a good part, Father John. Putting me to the test, checking that I am honest and true ... so I'm sorry about the deception. I had to find a way of getting you away from the monastery without people thinking you'd run off with a woman! You're safe here, Father John, for as long as it takes. I can tell you that you would *not* be safe carrying out your usual routine in and around the abbey, not at this moment. Believe me, this is for your benefit. You will be fully informed when it's all over. For the time being, please trust me.'

'I'm not sure what to think!'

'It was necessary to fool you for some of the time, sorry about that. I know it must be hard, believing me after what has happened, but I assure you this is for your ultimate benefit.'

'Is it to do with those child murders? You do have a look of that woman – their mum – but I don't even know your name! I know nothing about you.'

'I said you can call me Sue. It's not my real name but I'll respond to it.'

'Are you in the police?'

'Not the police.' She smiled briefly. 'But I'm not a criminal either.'

'You're not related to the Goddards, are you? You've such a look of Geraldine and I reckon you'd be about the same age.'

'You ask too many questions, Father John. There is no need to know anything about me. I'm a mature woman, not a youngster looking for romance and excitement. I am looking after you, you have your own bed-room – small, I grant you, with not much of a view but it's comfortable and quiet. And safe. The bathroom is adjoining, you have a TV, radio and books to keep you occupied – and there has been no broadcast about your disappearance. That is what I want. No news is good news so far as I am concerned. You are able to fulfil your priestly obliga-tions. I shall not object to that or try to pre-vent you. And I shall ensure you are cared for and well fed. You will be comfortable and you will be safe. Consider yourself a lodger for the time being. When the proverbial coast is clear, I shall return you to Maddleskirk Abbey, safe and well, and no worse for your experience.'

'How will I get back to Maddleskirk Abbey?'

'I will see to that.'

'Am I right in thinking no one but you knows where I am?'

'Absolutely right.'

'You've not rung the abbey to say I'm safe? Won't they be looking for me?'

'I've not been in touch and have no intention of doing so – calls can be traced, even from mobile phones. And yes, the police – and your colleagues – will be searching for you.'

'Surely there has been something in the papers about my disappearance?'

'I've not seen any reports, Father John, nor heard anything on the news. Maybe everyone thinks you're in hospital? That's not the least bit newsworthy!'

'Maybe they don't want to raise the alarm in case it causes more concern and undue publicity? I've been labelled a violent and evil man, Sue, but I am not. I shall not attack you or try to secure my release by violence. All I want to know is where I am, why am I here and when can I leave?'

'As I've often said, you'll be told everything in due course, rest assured.'

'So what day is it? I've lost track.'

'Tuesday. I have to go out soon to get some groceries so I'll get you a newspaper. But as usual I shall lock you in.'

'Even if you let me out to go shopping with you, I would not run away.'

'I can't risk that, and I can't risk anyone

recognizing you.'

'If I really knew what was going on, I'm sure I could co-operate much more effectively if it's all for my own benefit...'

'All in good time.' And she left, locking him securely in his room, but he did have a kettle full of water, some milk, a mug and a jar of instant coffee. But no telephone and no views from which he could attract attention. He was prepared for a long solitary wait – after all, he'd had plenty of practice in prison.

If he really wanted to escape he could do so – he'd learnt a few tricks in prison. But at the moment he had no wish to do that – he wanted to see this strange affair through to a successful conclusion.

In the rear of the cop shop at Maddleskirk Abbey, Nick had completed his examination of Father John's files, re-checking several times as a means of properly understanding their import. John's sketches of the interiors and exteriors of the houses showed something that the investigating detectives had clearly not considered relevant. Several lofts along the terrace of twenty-five houses had been linked – it was possible for a medium-sized person and certainly a child to crawl along the length of most of the terrace by using the lofts. Some householders had blocked that route through their own

217

properties while others relied upon stoutly securing their loft doors to prevent access by burglars, trespassers and voyeurs.

In many Manchester streets of this type, burglaries and even rapes had been reported before those access routes had been made safe. Now the entire terrace with its two shops and houses had been demolished to accommodate a new road link with the A57(M).

From John's very comprehensive notes, aided by his building experience and then clarified and computerized by Father Will, it became evident that Michael Goddard could have secretly crawled from the off licence via that extended loft and gained entry to his own house through the loft door, deliberately left unlocked. He could then have killed the girls in their beds and escaped by the same route. The question was how could he have secretly got into the off licence loft to make that trip? And why do so when he had access to his own house at all times?

Locked in his prison cell, John had relied upon his memory to recapture the scene and it had been his builder's knowledge that reminded him of the extensive linked lofts. And he had recalled another important factor. Michael Goddard did not pop out to the off licence merely to obtain cans of beer – he had another reason.

On occasions he worked there in the evenings, stacking shelves and assessing the stocks to determine when or whether replacements were necessary. He also cleaned litter from the sales area and did other odd jobs. However, he was not paid in cash – the off licence did not generate much profit and in any case its owner did not want the hassle of formally employing someone, so Michael was paid in kind. His 'wages' would be cans or bottles of beer, lager, cider, stout or anything else he fancied. He was quite happy with that arrangement which helped to maintain his desired image of a family man with an ordinary house, wife and small family. That appeared to work and he'd always sought ways of earning a little extra cash for his family. The off licence was a modest help and he was sensible enough not to try stealing from it. John knew all this because he would often pop along to buy himself a few cans during the week.

What John had discovered was that the open lofts of that terrace of houses included the off licence but not the corner shop further along the street. Gossip in the locality had often talked of young thieves clambering along the lofts in the hope of descending into the off licence, but its owner, Stan Moore, was aware of the risks and kept his loft door firmly secure.

As a teenager, Michael Goddard had been one of those youngsters, so he knew the secret route from the off licence right along into his own home. If only his boss would forget to lock that loft door, Michael could have nicked enough booze to keep him going for years!

But the last thing Stan Moore always did before locking up was to check the loft door. He was sure no one would enter via that route when the shop was shut. John, living nearby, knew all about such goings on even if the murder detectives had failed to investigate that route. So had John told the investigating team about the loft during his questioning? The files did not answer that question. Later, sitting alone in his prison cell, John had struggled to recall the routine of the off licence and its customers, the work done there by Michael Goddard, and then the precise sequence of events on the night of the murder. And he had written them all down, scratching out words that required amending when more trustworthy memories came to him. The governor and warders had allowed him paper and pens – he told them he was writing a novel and had promised a copy for the prison library when it was published.

Whilst working on his papers, John's memory had been constantly stimulated. He recalled that fateful day over and over again. Geraldine Goddard had seen him in the street and asked if he would keep an eye on the girls that evening. This was a regular occurrence – the Goddards went out quite a lot and John, living on his own after his wife's death, was happy to oblige. Geraldine had said she was going out with her sister to celebrate their birthdays and would be leaving the house at 7 p.m. She had added that Michael would be in the house until later in the evening when he would pop out to the off licence as usual, sometimes to work and sometimes to collect a pack of six beer cans. Or do both. He would give the curious signal to John as he passed his window – three sharp raps on the glass – to announce his departure.

It meant the girls would be on their own for a while as Michael worked, and John would go around to the house and sit with them, not in their bedroom but downstairs, until one or other of the parents came home.

If they went to bed, however, he would look in on the girls from time to time to make sure they were both all right. And that's what he had done that night.

Since then, Father John had gone over and over those events, wondering how – and more recently why – he could have been wrongly accused of murdering the two little girls. That fateful afternoon, Mrs Goddard had asked him to sit with them, to which he had agreed. Firm to her promise, she had left the house at seven o'clock. John could not be sure of the precise time he'd heard the three raps on his window to announce Michael's departure but it meant the girls were alone. John could pop in whenever he wanted, just to make sure they were all right. He had a spare key.

However, another factor had crept in that night.

Stan Moore, owner of the off licence, had been ill with some kind of stomach problem. John had been told this by an old friend who had visited him in prison. Stan had asked a friend, a woman, to run the shop that evening – she'd done so previously and knew the routine. When Michael had turned up at the off licence, she might not have realized why he was there, hence her uncertainty about times. Michael would have told her he had come to do some work in the storage and sales areas, stacking shelves and so forth, a regular chore. Much of his work was out of her sight and she had left him to his own devices because it was evidently a regular job and he knew what he was doing.

John had reasoned that if Michael had been determined to kill the two girls – and John knew he was not their natural father – then he could have entered the loft above the off licence without that assistant's knowledge and crept along to his own house to descend minutes later via his own prepared loft ladder to commit his crime. Likewise, he could have returned to the off licence to resume his work without the assistant being aware of his short absence.

And if he had said goodnight to the assistant before returning home, his alibi would be complete. She'd think he had been working in the off licence all that time.

As Nick studied the papers, it seemed that John's interpretation of events was feasible, except for one important matter. Wouldn't Michael and/or his clothing have been bloodstained? So could he have washed himself or removed his clothes before returning to the off licence? Or stripped off his clothes before killing them? And bathed afterwards? Had the police searched his house for bloodstains other than in the children's bedroom? There was no record of such a search. Clearly the police did not suspect Goddard; although he had been interviewed for elimination purposes, his alibi withstanding their scrutiny. The woman in the off licence stated he'd been there all evening until leaving for home and those times corresponded with Goddard's discovery of John in the blood-soaked room.

Thereafter, all the suspicion had been directed against John, who was regarded as a secret paedophile who had violently silenced his victims.

So if Goddard had killed the girls, what was

his motive? That had never been discussed – and there was nothing in John's papers to suggest one – but it must have been a powerful one for even an evil man like Goddard to have committed such a dreadful act.

Nick recalled that John had thought someone else was in the Goddards' house that evening when he was there – he thought he'd heard a toilet being flushed downstairs. Was Goddard then in his own house and had he flushed away some evidence? The police had found nothing. Or had Goddard disposed of bloodstained items and other evidence in the off licence waste bins?

As Nick read the papers, he knew John had a good case for an appeal or even a pardon. But, he reasoned, the innocence of Father John did not prove the guilt of Michael Goddard or his wife. Had someone else killed the children? If so, why?

Just as Nick reached the end of Father Will's succinct summary, the little monk entered.

'Finished, Nick?'

'Just.' He nodded. 'And as you said, this does alter the situation somewhat even if there is no evidence to prosecute either of the Goddards.'

'Father John suggested something else, Nick. He claimed Goddard had killed his wife's two little girls because their father was a rival drug dealer who had double-crossed him. It was a most savage revenge but God-dard is known to have killed rivals, always without leaving any evidence to convict him. This was different. His revenge was to kill his rival's *children* – without his wife knowing of his guilt.'

'How did John come to know that?'

'He was told by a fellow prisoner. That theory, as a powerful motive, was never investigated.'

Chapter 16

Detective Chief Superintendent Napier wel-comed Nick and Father Will into his cramped office, offering the monk the spare chair and Nick a stool.

'This place isn't suited for big men at big meetings,' he said, grinning. 'But it's fine for small and short important meetings. So what have you got to tell me?'

'Before I begin, Mr Napier, is there any further news of Father John?' asked Nick.

'Nothing very dramatic but there is some-thing I can tell you,' admitted Napier. 'I'll do this first because it's relevant and could be termed our official line.'

'You make it sound like some kind of devious plot!'

'There are times when we've got to be devious if we want results, Nick.' There was a thin smile on Napier's lips. 'This is one of those times. I want others – even my own staff – to believe the official line whilst keeping the true situation under wraps, if only for a while. I do have my reasons.'

'This sounds complicated!'

'It's not as difficult as it seems and your police experience will have told you that such tactics are not uncommon. Anyway, the latest on Father John. We know he arrived at Scarborough Beach Hospital at the time he made known, but there he was met by a woman who hailed a taxi. It took them to Scarborough railway station – and from there, we have no further information. I should add that we have no reason to believe he has come to any harm.'

'You're still searching for him?'

'Officially we are. Our line is that we want to speak to the woman who met him and then hired the taxi. Local CID is chasing up that enquiry around Scarborough – without realizing it, they are spreading our "official" line.'

'Has the taxi been traced?'

'It has, and the driver's been interviewed, but he can't tell us much. He did say that the woman paid the fare before entering the railway station. From there, the trail goes cold. That is the official line. For your own information, Nick, I can say that Father John is safe and in hiding, and I can confirm he has not had a romantic rendezvous with that woman!'

'So we say he was kidnapped?'

'That's the impression we want to give. By getting the local police to hunt for him in Scarborough, we are stirring up the local villains who want us off their backs, so some might also be looking for him, just to get some relief from being questioned. Word of that should reach our targets via some of those villains. It's our way of announcing John is in Scarborough. That might attract the attention of people of interest to us.'

'So how does this affect the murder of the man in the wood?'

'No more progress on that one. We've a team researching the background of the victim now we know his name and his job. I am stifled by official secrets at the moment but the official version is that the reason for him being in this locality remains a mystery. The Met is also deliberately keeping quiet about it. In our case, we're conducting detailed enquiries in and around the abbey and in nearby villages, using my officers and the monkstables as we try to establish any sightings. Apart from Greengrass's sighting we've no other reports of him being seen before he died, with or without a companion. We want to continue the impression we have not had a breakthrough. Meanwhile, to create something of a smokescreen, Inspector Lindsey and his team are still somewhere in the York area making a fuss about trying to trace the Goddards.'

'So we are very busy, away from here?'

'I am known for not hanging about, Nick! Whilst all this is going on, my officers are visiting criminals throughout the area, questioning them about their recent movements and so on. It's a useful smokescreen. You can't beat stirring the hornets' nest from time to time! It's a way of getting the criminal fraternity rattled – getting us off their backs by providing useful information about the Goddards.'

'Your sting operation? The Serious Rumour Squad at work!'

'That's it, Nick! Things are a bit slow but it's early days and we're getting there. I remain optimistic. I'm not called Nabber Napier without reason! Usually, I get my man. Now, are you going to brighten my day with something good?'

Nick turned to Father Will. 'Father Will has been doing some good work – over to you, Father.'

'Thanks, Nick. Mr Napier, I've been through that box of papers we found under Father John's bed.'

'And have they produced anything interesting?'

'I believe so.' Father Will provided a detailed and very comprehensive account of what had been revealed, including a possible motive for Goddard killing the children. Napier listened intently, not interrupting but occasionally jotting notes on his pad.

When Will had finished, Napier asked, 'Has anyone else seen these papers or had access to this information?'

'Not to my knowledge,' confirmed the monkstable. 'Certainly not since we got possession of them. Father John had them under his bed, as you know, and since we obtained them, they've been locked in the cop shop. It's secure; no one can enter unless the place is staffed.'

'Those papers need to be kept very safe.'

'I realize that but Goddard's suggested motive is not in writing in those files – it was something John told me.'

'I can check with Manchester CID to see if there is any truth in that – they'll have records even if there was no prosecution. Now we need to keep the papers and his computer very secure,' Napier stressed. 'And I mean *very* secure. They could be dynamite in the wrong hands. Now, Father Will, do you know of any attempts to break into any private apartments at the monastery? In fairly recent times.'

'There are always people trying to get in, wandering visitors usually, who are keen to find out how the monks live. It's just ill-mannered curiosity, we believe, mostly nothing malicious. Usually it's nothing more than stupidity and rudeness. Nonetheless, we keep the entrance gate firmly closed at all times.'

'That must be an inconvenience?'

'Not really. The resident monks use a press-button code. It changes every day and we also have keys for our own rooms. The monks' cell doors are very solid and each has a five-point locking system – there are some valuable pieces of sculpture and art work in our rooms. They're owned by the abbey trustees, I might add, not by individual monks. We're just the custodians. They'd be too tempting for dishonest collectors if they were displayed in our public corridors.'

'Are you aware of any attempts to steal from the monks' rooms? Particularly recently? Forced entries maybe but even devious ruses to get into the rooms?'

'It has happened on occasions.'

'I'm talking about forcible entries, Father Will. Break-ins. Criminal attempts. As burglars or vandals might use?'

'I can't recall such an attempt, Mr Napier. Apart from the internal security measures, none of the cells has windows that overlook the grounds or open onto anywhere that might be accessible by the public. Our ground-floor cells overlook the cloister which has one exit gate into the grounds, but that is always locked. We monks value our privacy. That gate has also a coded lock.'

'You're very up to date with your security measures! I must come to have a look when I've a moment to spare.'

'We owe it to the fact that, somewhere in this country, there is a retired police officer who has set up his own security business specializing in monasteries, convents, abbeys, cathedrals, churches and so forth. He understands the problems we face.'

'So when did he make your monastery secure?'

'Some time ago, seven or eight years at a guess.'

'If I wanted to trace him for a chat, would that be possible? If so, how would I find him?'

'You could find out who he was from either the procurator or the estate manager. I don't know whether or not he is still operating.'

'No problem, I'll find him if I need to talk to him. Well gentlemen, this is most interesting – and most useful. You've opened my eyes and presented some highly important evidence. What a blessing Father John talked to you and committed his thoughts and conclusions to paper.'

'He and I are good friends, Mr Napier. We help each other. I should add that he has told me all about his past.'

'All of it?' Napier frowned.

'Well, I can't be sure of that, can I? But I'm sure he has told me as much as he wants me to know. About the murders, I mean. And the Goddards.'

'That's more like it.' Napier then drew a deep breath as if he was going to unburden himself. 'Now's the time to level with you fellows,' he said unexpectedly. 'I've told you a little about our strategy but now I feel you should know more. I say that because I know I can trust you both. You must keep to yourselves what I am going to reveal to you now but I think it will help if you know this.'

Nick glanced at Father Will, who appeared to be somewhat puzzled.

'We can keep secrets if that's what you're asking,' responded Father Will.

'As closely as you do in confession?' asked Napier.

'It's something we learn to cope with in my profession.'

'Me too,' responded Nick.

'When Nick joined the force, he would have to swear on oath under the Official Secrets Act that he can keep his mouth shut when he has to. Right, listen to this but don't repeat it, not to anyone. There is much more than meets the eye so far as this murder is concerned, and that applies also to Father John's disappearance. In view of what you've just told me, I believe you need to know more. Come along, we're going for a walk, all three of us.'

'Should Prior Tuck be informed of whatever you're going to tell us?' suggested Father Will.

'It's not necessary at this stage, Father Will. The fewer people who are aware, the better. I'm telling you because of your closeness to Father John. You especially, Father Will. What I'm about to tell you has direct links with him. Come along, fresh air beckons!'

Outside his office as they headed for the door of the murder room, he called over to Detective Sergeant Salkeld. 'Just going for a bit of fresh air, Sarge, a tour of the grounds for a few minutes. Listen out for my phone.'

'Right, boss.'

And so they walked into the balmy September sunshine as a warm breeze caused some colourful leaves to cascade from the maturing trees, and they blew across the well-tended playing fields and lawns to settle upon the pathways that skirted the edges.

'I could live here,' commented Napier. 'It's so calm and peaceful ... not at all like working in a busy police station where there's no time to stand and stare!'

'We monks have a reputation for finding the most peaceful places on earth!' said Will, smiling.

'And that takes skill and foresight, Father

233

Will. Now, is there somewhere we can sit and chat without attracting flapping ears? I want to tell you something that is both secret and important because I think it will help us all. I might add that some of my senior officers are unaware of this.'

'I'll honour your trust in us,' said Father Will.

'Me too,' promised Nick, adding, 'There are seats around the cricket field, it's quiet just now.'

'Show me.'

As the trio approached, they saw a solitary monk in his long black habit with the hood raised to hide his facial features as he walked smoothly around one of the distant rugby football pitches, head bowed as if in deep contemplation or prayer. With the abbey church in the background, it would have made an atmospheric photograph and so engrossed was the monk that he appeared totally unaware of their presence. He had been walking there in large circles around the circumference of the pitch long before they arrived and Napier felt he was far enough away not to overhear their conversation.

In any case, he was walking away from them – quite anonymous.

'Who is that? Any idea?' Napier asked Father Will.

'Not a clue, I'm sorry. We all look alike when we're dressed up like that! We look like hoodies! We don't wear our habits with hoods up – cowls in other words – when we're in public places, except inside a church. Not many people know that.'

'It's a very effective disguise,' commented Napier. 'Is he saying his prayers or working out a strategy for winning at rugby football during this new season?'

'Probably both,' replied Will.

They reached a seat well away from the cricket pavilion and nets, then settled down. Both Father Will and Nick waited in silence as Napier gathered his thoughts and the hooded monk disappeared among the pavilion and changing rooms.

'I don't need to go into the details of John's life and his conviction for an appalling murder of two little girls, you know all about that. However, since getting involved in this inquiry, I have spoken to the chief constable of Greater Manchester Police whose officers investigated the murders and to the governors of HM Prisons at Full Sutton in Yorkshire and Armley in Leeds where John served his sentence. I consider it to be of concern that all have expressed doubts about John's guilt.'

'I understand he couldn't be released on parole until he admitted his guilt?' said Nick.

'That's about it.' Napier nodded. 'While locked up, it would have been most difficult for him to arrange a retrial or defend himself;

none of his papers would be confidential, the warders would search everything. He had no privacy.'

'But he did confess to the crimes in the end,' Father Will added. 'It was a means of gaining some semblance of freedom. He has been out of prison for about ten years and a monk for around three. He is still bound by the conditions of his parole licence and needs professional advice and help if he's going to do battle with the courts and the appeals system.'

'John's predicament involves more than that,' Napier told them solemnly. 'To speak as if I was a policeman giving a quote to the press, I will say, "I have reason to believe that John's life is in great danger". And that is what concerns me, and why I think you should know. You've probably worked that out but I'm making it official. We must remain alert to the possibility of the danger coming from the real killer of children, gentlemen.'

'You're accusing Michael Goddard of murder, even without a trial?' asked Nick.

'Yes, I am, because he is a truly nasty piece of work, the worst of the worst. I know he did it, you know he did it. That's what drives us on.'

'So where is John now?' asked Nick. 'You seem to know. Who was the woman who tricked him into going off to hospital?'

'Let's go back a little further, Nick.' Napier spoke quietly and calmly. 'When John was doing his time in prison, he discovered how drugs were being smuggled into the jail and distributed to inmates. The prison staff, from the governor downwards, had always done their best to prevent deliveries but had failed. They couldn't find out how the stuff was getting past their security systems. John found out through his knowledge of the building trade. At the time he was working on a huge new development within the prison grounds, part of a new extension. It involved brickwork. Quite by chance, he discovered drugs were being smuggled into the prison inside imitation bricks that were hidden among genuine deliveries. John was working on the project and found such a brick. At first, he didn't understand what it was – he thought it might be a bomb so he alerted the governor.'

'I'd say that was a good move.'

'It was but it alienated some of the other inmates. It was tantamount to being an informer. But John was looking after himself – he had no wish to be accused of importing whatever was inside the bricks. John was – is – an honest man, and the prison authorities knew that. Because of his actions, a dealer outside the prison was set up in a sting operation and caught. The outcome was that for a while drugs were not delivered, the dealer got a two-year sentence and lots of inmates suffered withdrawal symptoms. Even though John had acted nobly by our standards, in prison he had to be kept in solitary confinement for his own safety. Some very vicious and ruthless prisoners were out to get him whilst outside the prison walls, that dealer – Goddard – is still seeking John, not only to get his revenge for that but also to prevent John from speaking further. Quite simply, John knows too much, and Goddard wants him silenced.'

'So John is being cared for?' asked Will.

'He is,' said Napier. 'I know where he is but must keep quiet a little longer. Goddard has recently come very close to finding John. His presence here as a monk has until now been an effective disguise. Now, it seems, his whereabouts have become known. Hence our complicated protection.'

'I can understand your manoeuvre in Scarborough but he is a genuine monk, isn't he?' asked Nick.

'He is,' agreed Father Will.

'This doesn't make sense, does it?' cried Nick. 'John would have been far safer left in prison even if he was in solitary the whole time!'

'John has never condoned drugs and he nurses an especial dislike of dealers who make big money out of the grief and misery of their customers. Whilst still in prison, John was approached to see if he would help in another sting operation to help to identify and catch not merely the outside dealer he'd encountered through the prison, but a network of others, including Goddard. A big, big job in other words. Even so, he could not appear to have been granted favours for his release, so it still required him to admit his guilt for those murders. Once he had done that, he would be released on licence on condition he helped to trap a large gang of dealers. John still had a bargaining point – he agreed to do that in return for his case being reopened. Examination of the court records and the prosecution files did cast doubt on his conviction, and consequently the Home Office gave its consent. The case for his innocence has not been heard yet in court but it can be reopened and will be helped by his private papers. You know what they contain. However, in the meantime, he is the bait in a rather sophisticated trap.'

'Does he know that?' asked Nick.

'He knows some of this and he is playing a good part. Remember we are dealing with vicious criminals who'll kill without remorse. All the risks were made known to John but he still agreed to go ahead albeit pretending he knows nothing. He was made aware of that hospital ruse, by the way, and agreed to go along with it. He's acting his part very well. Undercover agents are in

Scarborough, keeping an eye on things, watching local drug dealers especially.'

'A brave man, in other words?'

'Very. But as he said when he agreed, he has nothing to lose, has he? He does not want a life forever being pointed out as the man who killed two little girls – he's innocent and wants to be free of that stigma.'

'And this will help?'

'Yes, a lot. If John leads us to the high command of drugs dealing in this region, his mission will be half-complete. The second half will enable him to pursue the appeal against his conviction with all the professional help that he'll require.'

'I can't see how that will work,' puzzled Father Will.

'We believe the drugs tsar in these parts is none other than Michael Goddard, who has moved from Manchester under an alias. We are still trying to get our hands on him, although we do know a good deal about him and his activities. However, we still lack the evidence that is necessary to convict him of either drug dealing or the murder of those girls. After half a lifetime of useless and unsuccessful attempts at making money, he managed to turn himself into a very successful businessman and drugs dealer, even if it is unlawful. He is making mountains of money and we believe his overseas shipments, in and out of the country, are centred on one of those small bays near Scarborough. In the past, they were used for smuggling liquor, now it's drugs.'

'I thought the intelligence was that he was living near York and had established a thriving business there?' puzzled Nick. 'Something to do with manufacturing strong waterproof cases for mobile phones and so on.'

'We've established a strong presence in York to make him believe we are concentrating on that area, but we're not. It's all part of our decoy operation, in conjunction with other agencies. We will gain something positive by flushing out lots of minor villains.'

'Will it work?'

'We can never be a hundred per cent sure but we've got to give it a go. Word of our activities in York will reach him wherever he is, we'll make sure of that, but in truth we have good reason to believe the centre of his operations is Scarborough.'

'Because of its coastal situation?' asked Nick.

'Yes, it's a busy port with lots of tiny deserted coves along the coastline, all with easy illegal access to the continent. Anything big can come through Hull or Teesside, neither being far away. Our real concentration, even as we speak, is the coast, even if we are pretending otherwise.'

'So Father John is in Scarborough?' Nick wanted to clarify that situation.

'He is. We put him there, Nick. He's in a safe house in the care of a SOO – Special Operations Officer – and an assistant. She's not a police officer but our intention is to trap Goddard by throwing him completely off the scent as we bait a trap for him.'

'He'll be used to that sort of thing, won't he?' asked Father Will. 'Won't he suspect anything that's out of the ordinary?'

'Up to a point, yes,' admitted Napier. 'But we and our partner agencies are up to scratch. Now you can see why we don't want press interest. If the press publicized our big operation in York, Goddard would be suspicious ... he'd think it was a ploy to catch him off guard. We've got to convince him that that operation is low key so far as press interest is concerned, then he might believe it is genuine.'

'It all sounds very complicated,' admitted Father Will.

'It will all unravel itself eventually, but we've an extra ace in our hands. We still have Father John's box of notes to dangle in front of Goddard when the time is right – metaphorically speaking, of course. If he thinks someone has got a file of information that could prove he committed those child murders, he'll want to destroy it, as well as the man who created it. The man who can give evidence against him. Remember, this man is ruthless, highly dangerous and highly innovative. But we're going to nail him.'

'So did he kill Inspector Radcliffe, that undercover policeman?' asked Nick.

'Almost certainly. We're not going to interrogate him about that, not yet, but very soon we will be looking for a realistic holding charge to keep him in custody so we can question him – about drugs as well as the murder. Our thinking is that Radcliffe was getting very close to the truth and had to be eliminated by Goddard. I think the woman seen by Greengrass with Radcliffe near the holy well was Mrs Goddard. There was a crude attempt to implicate Father John in that death by leaving the murder weapon in the confessional – by chance at that time, it was occupied by you, Father Will.'

'Oh dear ... how devious ... I could have been arrested...' he whispered hoarsely, 'but that was a woman...'

Memories of that occasion flashed before him as he spoke but in those fleeting moments Will wondered if that woman's confession had been genuine? If it was false, it might not be governed by the seal. Perhaps he could reveal what had been said? He'd have to check before he opened his mouth.

'Do you agree, Father Will?' asked Nick.

'Agree with what? Sorry, both of you, my

mind got distracted...'

'That the woman who attended your confession might not have been genuine in what she was doing, and she might have been the wife of Michael Goddard?'

'I can't say, I didn't see her – she was no more than a silhouette against the mesh inside.'

'Did you get the feeling she was not a Catholic?' asked Nick.

'That could be possible. I felt she was not accustomed to going to confession She seemed rusty and not at all comfortable in there. She might not have been genuine.'

'Maybe she'd seen scenes of someone making their confession in a television play or something,' contemplated Napier.

'But why would she do that?' asked Nick. 'Why leave the murder weapon there?'

'Firstly, as a means of exerting pressure on Father John,' said Napier. 'Making him appear to be involved in the death of Detective Inspector Radcliffe – you can be sure she would make sure the stiletto was discovered, perhaps by a cleaner. It would have implicated the man she thought was taking those confessions who was also a convicted murderer – and a danger to her husband and to her. From this, it's obvious the Goddards have discovered the whereabouts of John, and his new name, even if they don't know exactly which of the monks is him.'

'We all look like penguins in our habits!' laughed Will.

'It was clear that Mrs Goddard did not know John in his new guise. That was clearly displayed at the confessional. Father Will, you have probably helped to prevent a murder. Well, now you're in possession of more information than most others so what do you see as our next task?'

'Surely it's to find Goddard?' suggested Nick.

'No,' said Napier. 'It's to draw him gently into our net without him realizing, and then catch him red-handed with drugs in his possession or evidence strong enough to get him convicted. But capturing him is more important than finding any drugs. Following that, we can inform him that we have reason to believe he killed his own stepdaughters. He'll be kept in custody as we gather the evidence.'

'You sound very sure about all this, Mr Napier?' Nick put to him.

'We're coming to the climax of a lot of work. Sadly we didn't anticipate Inspector Radcliffe's death, but it does show what's at stake. We're keeping that in the background at this stage – we're going to build a massive case or cases against him before he's arrested. I should add that we do know where he lives, and we know the name of his new business in this area. We've done a lot of background work on this case. In short, gentlemen, that man is finally going to pay for his sins.'

'He's not the sort to readily confess,' suggested Nick. 'To sins or crimes!'

'And not to me or to you, Father Will, he's not a Catholic. We checked that when our undercover agents discovered his unhealthy interest in Maddleskirk Abbey. Because he will never confess to anything, we need the strongest evidence to convict him. Now I must get back to my office – the teams will think I've deserted them and it must be nearly tea-time. I could murder a cuppa.'

Chapter 17

'What are your plans now?' asked Napier as they walked back to the abbey.

'There doesn't seem to be much to involve us any more,' admitted Nick. 'We're very much on the fringes of all this. We mustn't and shouldn't get involved in your complex plans, Mr Napier. We could make a mess of things. It seems our efforts in and around the abbey, not forgetting the villages here-abouts, are now complete – we've done all we can. We've exhausted local enquiries without finding much that's useful to your investigation.'

'You and your monkstables, especially Father Will, have been very useful to my teams, Nick, as I'm sure you understand. It's all part of the diversion plan. Your efforts meant my officers were able to concentrate elsewhere but there's still something that can be done by the monkstables,' suggested Napier.

'Such as?'

'A high-profile search for Father John on the moors.'

'But you know where he is.'

'We do, but no one else does. Everyone else is worried about him and expecting some kind of positive and highly visible action to find him. We've not resorted to a big public search so it's time we did. I suggest you recruit help from the police dog section, the Moorland Search and Rescue Service, members of the public and even a helicopter. There are enough woodlands, forests and lakes around here to keep a search team busy for hours if not days! If there are any fees or costs, my murder investigation budget will cover them. That would be a wonderful way of diverting public interest – and Goddard's interest – from what is actually happening, and the public will expect something of that kind. Who knows what or who we might flush out!'

'Something nasty?'

'It's rather like going beating on a grouse

shoot! You never know what's going to blast out of the heather!'

Nick wondered whether Napier had been inspired by the sight of that monk striding around the grounds in his habit but felt he should agree.

'I must admit I thought things were rather low key.'

'Not any more, Nick. All we need to get this show moving is a reported sighting of a monk in an isolated location. That would give *us* grounds for a search.'

'And it would attract media interest,' pointed out Nick. 'I thought you didn't want that?'

'We do now! It will have its uses because it will divert interest from what we are actually doing. Word of our activities will soon filter down to the media,' said Napier. 'I can live with a staged media event. A big search for a missing monk will guarantee that. The public and news reporters will think we're chasing a murderer, which guarantees wide coverage.'

'We've already exhausted enquiries around the abbey campus and the villages in the first search for Father John...'

'That was yesterday, Nick. Now, how will this work? Suppose I arranged for an anonymous phone call ostensibly from a hiker who's out on the moors with someone else's wife which is why he refused to give his name? However, he's heard about the missing Father John due to our local searches and enquiries and has rung to report the sighting of a monk wandering about as if lost on, say, moors near Whinstone Ridge? That's not too far from here. Let's say he was dressed in his hooded habit ... but with no rucksack or walking gear. An elderly confused monk in danger of exposure along with all that that brings. We can express our concern because these autumn nights can be very cold – so this is a life-saving exercise.'

'Isn't that a bit devious?' frowned Father Will. 'Concocting a story like that?'

'I've known many a serious crime be solved through the initial stimulus of an anonymous phone call or an anonymous letter,' said Napier.

'I thought most were ignored?' suggested Nick.

'As a rule they are but in this case it's all for the greater good. It's all part of our plan to divert the target's attention from Scarborough and the coast and it means we can call off the hunt any time we wish. There's no need to let it get out of hand or become too expensive. How about a highly visible but reasonably short search?'

'I'll go along with that,' promised Nick.

'We might even get a sighting! If that happened, it could lead to our target joining the search – remember, he's as anxious as we are to find Father John.'

'I don't think my conscience will permit me to go along with those plans,' Father Will added with a rueful smile, 'but if a search does develop because of reports that Father John's been genuinely sighted, then I'll be pleased to help.'

'Imagine the public interest if we get a fine body of monkstables in their police uniforms helping to search the moors and forests for one of their fellows who is missing,' mused Napier. 'An elderly monk in distress who might have wandered off whilst suffering from dementia. There'd be huge public sympathy with volunteers offering to join the search. And bags of publicity.'

'Do we name the missing monk?' asked Nick.

'In this case we do,' confirmed Napier. 'We'll be quite clear that we *believe* it to be Father John Attwood who's been missing since Saturday. There's no need to be more specific. Once we've planted the first seeds of his unexplained absence, it's quite feasible he might have gone for a walk and got lost.'

'But his last sighting was near the entrance to Scarborough Beach Hospital,' Nick pointed out. 'We can positively place him there after leaving the abbey around five on Saturday evening – the hospital denies he was admitted.'

'All fodder for our media friends!' laughed Napier.

'There are places near Whinstone Ridge where we could search for him,' Father Will explained. 'I know it well. Just below the summit there's an old disused chapel but it does have walls and a roof but no doors or windows, just gaps. Hikers and ramblers often use it for shelter, and sometimes it's full of sheep sheltering from the weather. It's called St Aiden's Chapel, pilgrims used to trek up there. The name of Aidensfield is from the same source and I do know that some of our monks go up there when they want to escape hoards of visitors at the abbey.'

'It sounds perfect,' said Napier. 'That will become our operational base. Good, that's settled. Return to the Postgate Room and I will set things in motion. Go there ostensibly for a cup of tea and a biscuit, and I'll contact you once I've got things moving. You'll then have to alert Friar Tuck and his merry men who will join the search. I'll have the inspector in charge of this division drafted in to lead the search – he'll think it's genuine and I'll instruct him to bring in some of his own officers and equipment and he will also seek help from the Moorland Search and Rescue, the RAF Search and Rescue and anyone else he can think of. All such organizations will alert the press. And whilst you're involved in those diversionary tactics, we shall be extending our web, hopefully to catch a very big and very nasty fly!'

In his lonely room with no view, Father John occupied himself by delving into local history books as the woman called Sue busied herself downstairs, sometimes chatting to a colleague whom he never saw.

As someone holding him prisoner, she was very considerate, he felt, visiting every hour or so to offer cups of tea, small meals and other things to keep him occupied. He had a pack of cards to play patience and there were board games by which he could challenge himself such as Scrabble. All the things you'd find in a holiday flat. He was also pleased his room had *en suite* facilities, and that he could lock his bedroom door.

In some ways he felt very much a wimp being held captive by a woman even if she was armed and had a companion at hand. But John was not the sort of man who would attack a woman or attempt to overcome her by force – such actions could be misconstrued. To reinforce her own security and safety, she kept all doors locked with no keys visible, including the solitary outer door – all had mortise locks which meant he could not unlock them without the keys. Also, he noted his windows were double glazed against the

North Sea's fury and firmly locked. There seemed to be no telephone cables in the flat – Sue had a mobile she often used. When things were quiet he could hear her on her phone downstairs although he could not decipher her words. She received a lot of calls but very infrequently made any; he guessed it was her controller monitoring the situation. On the occasions she did enter his room, he would attempt to find out how long he would remain and what was expected of him. Despite volunteering to help, he had not been told much about all this! He knew a little of what was going on, but not everything.

'You can keep asking me questions, Father John, but I cannot give you answers. I do not know what is going to happen or how long you will be there. But you are comfortable, there is food and shelter, and you have a bed. Please try to be patient. Consider me your guardian, not your captor. I am keeping you safe.'

'I can do that, I don't really want to know what's going on. It's a bit like living in the monastery. And it reminds me of my prison cell, not knowing what lies ahead.'

'Then settle down and enjoy as much of it as you can while you can. Please don't try to stage an escape, Father John, it wouldn't be wise. I am always armed but if it's any consolation, I think our realistic play-acting could soon be over.'

Alone with his thoughts and now thinking wistfully about his pleasant room at the monastery, he wondered what his colleagues would be doing. He'd told Father Will he was coming to Scarborough Beach Hospital but as he had not booked in and not returned to the abbey, would there now be a search? By the monkstables? If so, where would they be looking – and would they search his room hoping for clues as to his whereabouts? If so, who would conduct the search? They'd need the abbot's consent to enter his room, but not if the police had a search warrant! When receiving that call about his urgent visit to hospital, he'd not had time to write it in his diary, so no one would know about it. Except Father Will, of course. So what had Will done, apart from hear confessions? Had anyone checked at Scarborough Beach Hospital? And if they had searched his room for clues, would they have found his box of papers?

Father John had been told very little about this operation, other than not to mention the truth to anyone. He hoped he could maintain the pretence. Father Will knew about that box but could Will be trusted? Who could you trust these days? He thought of his time in prison when no one, absolutely no one, could be trusted and that business with the drugs had made him hated by the inmates – and some warders! Those papers held his innermost thoughts about his conviction and might be his key to a successful appeal. Were they safe now he was not using his room?

If they got into the hands of the Goddards and their Mafia-like family, they would destroy them – that was a certainty. Was it possible to break into the monastery to steal those papers? Did Goddard know he had compiled such a file? But how *could* he know?

And, of course, it was the Goddards who were the drugs tsars, using ways of secretly distributing heroin, cocaine and cannabis resin into most of the British prisons and other detention centres, and to a range of other outlets. They were using the building trade as their cover – hiding the stuff in hollowed-out bricks and timbers. Via the proverbial grapevine, he'd heard the Goddards, Michael and Geraldine, were now multimillionaires through their drug dealing and were operating from a base near Scarborough under another guise and another name. But he did not know those names or identities.

As he sat alone, brooding about his past, he wondered how Michael could have summoned the necessary mental state to kill those innocent children, whatever the reason. Was he under the influence of drugs at the time? What was his personal state of health, mental or otherwise, or his wealth, at the time of the murders? Father John knew that Michael Goddard had not been successful in his younger days; life had been a struggle both financially and emotionally. There were times when Father John, then known as John Jacobson and retired from the building trade, had lent him money, not expecting it to be repaid. He knew the Goddards had considered him their trusted friend – now he had paid the penalty.

His thoughts turned more and more towards the Goddards; now they were 'highly successful' and wealthy drug dealers, did they see him as a threat? And the woman who was holding him in this flat – she had a look of Mrs Geraldine Goddard.

She would have aged since those days, of course, but she'd gone out that fateful evening ... with her sister. To celebrate *their* birthdays. So were they twins? Like the little girls? Did twins run in her family? But if she *was* related to the Goddards, could he trust her? Had he, in fact, fallen into a trap?

Father John sat on the edge of his bed staring out of the viewless window onto a solid brick wall. Bricks, he thought. Did they contain heroin? Cocaine? Cannabis? Not those actual bricks but others just like them. It gradually seemed more and more likely that he might be the victim of a highly elaborate hoax. Or some kind of secret operation! So who could he trust?

Then there was a light knock on his door, a key was placed in the lock and it opened. Sue was there with a tray bearing a cup of tea and some chocolate biscuits and brought them in with a smile. She placed the mug and plate of biscuits on his dressing table as she said, 'Deep in thought, were you? Or perhaps asleep? I had to knock twice.'

'Deep in thought,' he answered.

'Can I ask what you were thinking?'

'I was wondering if you are the sister of Geraldine Goddard. Jenny is her name? Her twin, in fact? Is that you?'

'Whatever gave you that idea, Father John?' She quickly left the room with no further comment.

By chance, Prior Tuck was in the Postgate Room when the phone rang. It was Detective Chief Superintendent Napier. 'Can you get all the monkstables together, please, Friar Tuck? In quarter of an hour? I need to talk to them. And include Nick Rhea.'

'Yes, no problem. Can I ask why?'

'I've a big job for them, a search area to check out.'

'Understood.'

And so it was that the monkstables gathered once more for a briefing; Nick was with them as Napier burst in and asked them to be seated.

'Thanks for mustering so quickly,' he praised them. 'My own officers would have taken far longer to get organized. Now this is the situation. We've had reports of a sighting of a lone monk on Whinstone Ridge, near the old chapel of St Aiden. The call came from a hiker who rang the control room at police headquarters from a kiosk. He refused to give his name because he's sneaking off work and away from his wife for a day out with his girlfriend. They spotted the monk up near the chapel, an old man as he was described, looking lost or bewildered. Oddly, he was wearing his habit with the hood raised, and seemed distressed. That was about twenty minutes ago. He wondered if the monk was from this abbey so the call was transferred to me because of our ongoing enquiries. However, the caller rang off before I could get more details such as the time he saw the monk or whether or not he was injured. From the tone of his conversation he seemed a down-to-earth person with a local accent and I have no reason to believe it is a hoax or a false alarm with good intent. Search and rescue teams are being called out; they're always keen to have practical experience. An experienced team of police officers will also conduct a search and we shall join them. If we don't find him, we'll consider the use of police dogs or even a helicopter. The RAF Search and Rescue team might use theirs; if they do, they will refer to it as an exercise. It means you must all head up to that location immediately and get yourselves organized into a search party. Assemble at the ruined St

Aiden's Chapel, it's on the map.'

He paused to allow them a few moments to digest his words, then added,

'A local police inspector – Inspector Carter – is on his way and he will be in overall charge. Make yourselves known to him. You have transport?'

'We have our own personnel carrier,' said Prior Tuck.

'Right, on your way! I've spoken to the abbot and he agrees that you should join the search. I will be in touch with the inspector-in-charge by radio during the search. If it does prove to be Father John, let me know as soon as possible but bear in mind he has been missing since Saturday and might require hospital treatment. Also, if he has been dossing down in that old chapel, we need to know whether he was alone – there may be signs of multiple occupancy or the remains of food and so on.'

'Can I ask one thing?' asked Nick Rhea.

'Shoot but be quick!' said Napier.

'Will the press be informed?'

'Yes, I've spoken to the force press officer and he is issuing an immediate news release via the Press Association so that all newspapers, radio and TV stations, local and national, are aware of this search. We've also issued a fairly recent photo of Father John taken last year when he was repairing an old dry stone wall in the grounds. In addition we need to search this immediate locality in case Father John has made his way back to the abbey. It all means he could be in danger and, as he's been missing since Saturday, he could be ill, mentally or physically – so do your best.'

And so Prior Tuck, map in hand, instructed his team to equip themselves with suitable clothing and footwear for a moorland search. They made a swift search of all likely places in the abbey and its surrounds with no result and then the prior led them out to the abbey transport department where a personnel carrier was waiting.

Prior Tuck ordered, 'Whinstone Ridge as fast as you can, Stan, and try to get as close as possible to St Aiden's Chapel – some of the tracks up there aren't very good for motor vehicles.'

The driver understood. 'I know the old chapel.' He smiled. 'Hang on to your hats, we're off!'

Chapter 18

'Have you seen this?' Geraldine shouted to her husband, who was working in his study.

'Seen what?'

'There's a big search underway on the

260

moors – police, rescue services and others – all looking for an old monk who's missing. It's on the news.'

Michael left his work for a moment, going through to the small lounge where the local TV news was being broadcast. He stood and watched as the camera highlighted a search party with dogs making their way across the moors. Others, men and women, with protective clothing bearing the name 'Moorland Search and Rescue' were doing likewise in the distance, and there were police officers searching in the background.

'Why do you think I'm interested in this?' he asked.

'Two reasons. First, you're always telling me you're keen to take advantage of opportunities for advertising with our helicopter. It's got to earn its keep, you keep telling me. So why don't we offer to help with that search? Free of charge. If we don't get in there first, some other enterprising businessman will beat us to it. If this search continues, Michael, you might get *Linneymoor Ceramics* on television. Think of all that free advertising! That must be worthwhile even if it's only on the regional news but some of these big searches can get national coverage. It's in our patch of Yorkshire too! And secondly it would establish us as decent people who are willing to help the community. It's important for us to gain some kudos and get accepted by the locals. You've always said you want respect from ordinary people.'

'Yes I do but do you honestly think it's a good idea, getting involved in matters of this kind? High-profile events? With those coppers all around and an audience that might contain rivals who'll try to take me out? You never know what might happen if we stick our heads too far above the battlements!'

'Michael, have I ever given you bad advice? Our legitimate business needs to appear legitimate! Openly legitimate, especially in the public eye. I've always been at your side, guiding you in our private and business life, making sure you do the best for both of us. This is another of those opportunities we can't afford to miss. All businesses big and small want to publicise themselves. And what about those air ambulances? You see them all over the place, rescuing people or taking injured people to hospital. They're supported by charity, like the lifeboats – people are prepared to dig deep into their pockets at the sight of a helicopter doing charitable work. That kind of image is now within our reach, Michael.'

'I don't want to look like a dim-witted big-head showing off his wealth! That can happen, you know. People can be very jealous, and we don't want that. You never know what it might lead to: bad things, too much exposure ... risky exposure. We're fairly new here, remember, we want to settle in and become an accepted part of the community. We don't want people to freeze us out of their lives just because of boasting we've got money and success. Acceptance is important to me.'

'Exactly, and that's why I think this would be a good idea. You'd be seen to be helping the community in a very humane exercise. We – the business, I mean – can only benefit from this and you'd be doing a real service to the community. Trust me, Michael.'

'You've got a point, I'll grant you that. So who is the chap they're looking for?'

'That's the real reason we should help. He's an elderly monk from Maddleskirk Abbey, he's not been seen since Saturday. He's Father John Attwood.'

'Attwood? Are you sure? Why would a helicopter be needed to look for him?'

'He's wandering and vulnerable. I thought you'd want to rescue him!'

'You don't really mean *rescue*, do you? Catch might be the better word. Yes, I would like to get my hands on him – so where was he seen? It seems your confession and stiletto trick flushed him out ... wonderful, wonderful ... just what we need. This might be the perfect opportunity to catch him, to deal with him once and for all. We'll never get another chance like this. OK, I'm convinced. What next? Remember I have a consignment to deliver later today.'

'That can wait. There's an old ruined chapel on those hills, St Aiden's Chapel, and according to the news they think he might have been sleeping rough there. Then it seems he got lost. He's not been seen since Saturday until today when he was spotted by a hiker near the old chapel. They think he's lost and wandering – you can easily get lost on those moors, Michael, they're wild and inhospitable with very little shelter, very dangerous for an old man. You need to show sympathy for him.'

'Sympathy? After what he did to us!'

'You'd be seen as a very caring person, Michael, and I'm sure there are places safe enough for a helicopter to land. Others have been used in rescues and searches up there. There are acres of open space surrounded by coniferous forests.'

'But ours is not a search-and-rescue machine, Geraldine. We've no heat-seeking equipment and no space for a stretcher...'

'Now you're making excuses! It's a helicopter and it can fly low while searching. It can hover, it provides a good view from up aloft and I'm a good pilot – we'd just be looking for him! Helping the search. You and me. There's seating for two more passengers – ideal for a rescue attempt and perfect for us to pick him up and rush him off the hospital. By then, we'll have got him!

And remember this, Michael, I want him to suffer for what he did to my little girls. It's my time for revenge, my turn to put matters right. We've a radio and could say we're taking him to York Hospital but once away from there, we could dump him in the sea or somewhere ... we'd say he opened the door and fell out. He'd never be found if we weighted his body ... or we could tell the police we left him on the York helipad with a member of staff and don't know where he is now. It's the chance I've been waiting for, Michael. We can't let this pass without doing something so shall I ring the police and make an offer? We must act quickly.'

'I hope you know what you're doing! You realize I don't want to get too close to the police; they may know more about us than we believe. We can't get too involved in such rescues. If we do it once, we'll be expected to do it again.'

'We'll be lost among other searchers but the fact you volunteered will mark you as an honourable sort of chap, part of a public-spirited team.' She smiled knowingly. 'It's always worked before; you've always established your credentials to work your way into acceptance by the community ... people are not concerned how you make your money, Michael, just that you've got a lot and you're not afraid to spread it around for the benefit of others! It's a perfect way of concealing our true mission in life.'

He waited a long time before answering, then said, 'All right. Let's do it, it's always worked before. We can make it work again.'

And so Geraldine made the call.

Out on the moors, Inspector Carter's mobile phone buzzed. 'Carter,' he responded.

'Sergeant Tanfield, control room, sir,' responded a voice. 'We've a businesswoman on the line, she's offering a helicopter and pilot to help in the search for that monk.'

'What's the catch?' asked the inspector.

'Catch? None so far as I'm aware.'

'Who is she?'

Sergeant Tanfield told him, 'She's a director of Linneymoor Ceramics, name of Rachel Morton. Her husband Joe is her business partner. They're located in the Old Brickworks at Linneymoor – the 'copter's got "Linneymoor Ceramics" in big letters on both sides. Cream-coloured body with terracotta lettering.'

'She's after a bit of free advertising then? Well, so long as she understands we can't pay for its use, that the pilot and aircraft must be comprehensively insured and that all the air navigational rules are obeyed. And we need to liaise with Gold Command.'

'Leave that to me. She has promised that all the necessary conditions will be met. She will be the pilot and will bring documents to be checked.'

'Sounds OK. Do we know anything else about them?'

'Nothing, sir. They're new to the district but they've not come to the notice of the police. I did the usual CRO check.'

'Nothing more than that? No other checks?' asked the inspector.

'No, sir.'

'All right, it'll certainly be a big help but she must be told that the pilot must take orders from the officer-in-charge of the search with approval from Gold Command. If she agrees, I see no reason to refuse the offer. It could search a huge grid in the fraction of the time we'd do it on foot so it will need an observer on board. The pilot must be told we've had no further sightings of the monk. Tell her the control point will be the ruined St Aidan's Chapel near Whinstone Ridge on the North York Moors. It's on the map and with bags of space for a landing site.'

'I'll get her to take the chopper to the old chapel, say, within the hour, unless the monk is found in the meantime? The pilot and any crew will be fully briefed on arrival.'

'Right, I'll be there, I'll hear and see their approach.'

'Right, sir. I hope this proves valuable to your search.'

'I'll make sure it does, Sergeant!'

At that stage, Detective Chief Superintendent Napier had no intention of going to the search venue; his presence was needed in the murder room as new information was received and fresh problems arose. Most if not all of the incoming information was negative but it did serve to terminate various unproductive lines of inquiry.

Much depended upon the outcome of the forensic pathologist's examination of the remains of the murder victim but he considered it significant that, apart from his clothing, he had no personal belongings with none being found at the scene or elsewhere. It suggested his death was the work of an experienced assassin.

Professional villains knew how to conceal or destroy evidence but they'd left his clothing untouched and enquiries had established it had come from retailers in the area where the victim had lived.

It was a small matter but important when confirming his identity. The injuries to the body after death bore all the signs of a fall from a considerable height and so it was necessary to examine the scene again, this time concentrating on the ground at the summit of the nearby cliff.

Despite the apparent lack of positive progress, Napier was satisfied he knew the identity of Inspector Radcliffe's killer – the method of killing had revealed that even if it was normally used against other drug dealers. So had Radcliffe defected? Had he become involved with the dealers, working with them instead of against them? Lured by thoughts of wealth? It was something to consider very carefully.

His chief concern now was to ensure that the case against Michael Goddard for the double murder of the girls could be proven beyond reasonable doubt and that would require the reopening of the original investigation and the inquest. So where was Goddard and what was he doing these days? Had DI Radcliffe been working for him? Or even pretending to work for him? Had he got too close, with catastrophic results? As he pondered his next moves, he wondered about the progress of the search around Whinstone Ridge and called Inspector Carter.

'Napier here, Inspector. Just a check call to see what developments there've been in your hunt. You've contacted Gold Command, I take it?'

'Yes, sir, all's in order. We're in radio link with their control room.'

'Splendid, we must follow the rules – most of the time, that is! Any sign of Father John?'

'Not yet, no further reported sightings, no discarded clothes or signs of him dossing down in the old chapel. I wish that chap who reported it was around to be quizzed a bit more; we're not sure exactly where he spotted Father John.'

'It's a big open area, Inspector, so do your best. It's probably better to prove that he's not there instead of finding him dead or very ill.'

'We might be in a position to do that, sir, I've just had an offer of a helicopter from a firm trading as Linneymoor Ceramics.'

'Have you now? So what have you learned about them?'

'They appear genuine. A man and wife team, Joe and Rachel Morton from Linney-moor village deep in the moors. We've checked them out, they own the Old Brickworks in Linneymoor and have revived it to provide clay for their ceramics. It seems there's still a lot of good-quality raw material in the old clay pits and its perfect for making floor tiles, brooches, dishes, plates, gift boxes, garden ornaments, plant pots, table ornaments, teapots, chain pulls, bathroom fittings – you name it and they seem to make it in their distinctive ceramics. It sells well, even overseas.'

'And they can afford to run a helicopter from that village enterprise?'

'So it would seem, sir.'

'Then I'm in the wrong job! Why are they offering their machine?'

'Free publicity, I guess. They'll get their helicopter with its business logo in the newspapers and on television. And they might even find the missing man.'

'On the other hand, they might not,' muttered Napier, adding, 'When do you expect the 'copter?'

'Within the hour. The pilot is the owner's wife, Rachel Morton. He's called Joe. They need to refuel it and do the usual pre-flight checks before take-off.'

'Then I'll come along to meet the Mortons and their helicopter. They sound interesting people. If they arrive before me, persuade them to do a circuit or two over the area you've not covered, and let the media take its picture. I'll see you soon.'

Before doing anything else, Detective Chief Superintendent Napier found a quiet corner and called Inspector Lindsey on his mobile phone.

'Napier here, Brian. There are interesting developments. I think the Goddards have taken the bait. This is now much more than just a search. I suggest you terminate your business around York and get here as fast as you can. I'm heading for Whinstone Ridge, there's an old chapel of St Aidan up there. You'll find me somewhere nearby. If anyone – such as the media – asks what's going on, say we're searching for Father John Attwood and we've a helicopter joining the hunt.'

'Attwood? He's not there, is he?'

'Of course not, but our helicopter owners

271

don't know that.'

'I won't ask any more questions. Where shall I bring my team?'

'To the search area; we can always find them a job.'

'Wilco.'

Napier then returned to the murder room and asked Sergeant Salkeld to join him in his cramped office. He told her to close the door.

'Anything doing, Jane?'

'Nothing special, sir. All quiet in fact.'

'How about our Scarborough actions?'

'No sightings of the missing monk, sir. He's thought to be on the moors now.'

'Just what we need. There's a big search with a helicopter about to join us, but he's not there, Jane. At the moment, he's in Scarborough in a safe house, but I'm going to level with you. You need to know what's going on.'

'Shall I call off the Scarborough teams?'

'No, I've another task for them but it means a shift of emphasis. We need to have them making urgent enquiries into a company called Linneymoor Ceramics.'

'They've premises not far from Scarborough, I believe.'

'Right. It's owned and run by a couple called Joe and Rachel Morton, they have a factory in Linneymoor village, the Old Brickworks about twenty miles inland from Scarborough. It reminded me of the drug dealers who smuggled bricks into the prison where Father John was doing his time. They concealed the drugs inside some of the bricks, then John blew the whistle. Despite that, they are still active, Jane, and have moved their centre of operations. But they still seem to like making bricks, probably ornamental ones along with other things for tourists.'

'At Linneymoor?' she asked.

'Yes indeed. Intelligence shows they dispose of their products in Scarborough and other seaside resorts along that coast, probably from as far north as Redcar down to Bridlington in the south. I've had a look at their website and they make the sort of things you expect tourists to buy as souvenirs. Fashionable bricks along with cheap and cheerful stuff. Teapots, mugs, jewellery boxes, model animals, toilet chain pulls, you name it, they make it – and sell it, here and overseas. I think much of their overseas sales are despatched by boat from Scarborough – even meeting other boats somewhere at sea to exchange cargos.'

'Maybe they feel secure because there's no law against making trinkets and selling them overseas, is there? Is this an HM Customs operation?'

'If I told you that I suspect some of those ceramic packs might contain drugs – heroin, cocaine, cannabis resin...'

'Ah, I've been slow, haven't I?'

'Not particularly. After all, the business is to conceal their real trade. You can see now why this has been kept in the background of our enquiries so far. With Father John's unwitting help, we're setting up a sting operation that should net a few drugs, a couple of seasoned dealers and even a killer...'

'This is out of my depth, sir.'

'Nonsense! If you want promotion in the CID, you've got to think deeper than local villains stealing scrap metal, nicking cars or burgling houses. So this is what I want you to do, on my orders and in my name, all with the consent of Gold Command. And, I might stress, with a high degree of secrecy.'

'Need I write anything down?'

'No. There's always a risk of someone else coming across bits of paper like that. Now this is what you must do.'

Chapter 19

'Sue, it's Napier speaking from the incident room.'

'Your check code, please, Detective Chief Superintendent.'

'Charlie Oscar 2736.'

'How can I help?'

'It's urgent. We need Father John to be somewhere else, as soon as possible but certainly within the hour. Can you fix that with your controller and Gold Command?'

'I'm sure there will be no problem. Where do you want us?'

'A half hour's drive away.'

'No problem. The official car's here in the garage at the flat.'

'Good. We don't want any local bobbies stopping you!'

'They won't. Where do you want us to go? My boss and Gold Command will want to know.'

'Whinstone Ridge, it's on Eltering Moor to the south of Aidensfield, lofty and deserted but with dense woods on the lower reaches, coniferous and deciduous. Ideal for concealing people, dead or alive. There's an old chapel on the plateau at the top and we're using it as our base. Teams of experienced searchers are assembling. There'll also be a search helicopter bearing the logo of Linney-moor Ceramics; it's been offered free of charge. Its ETA is within the hour.'

'Now that name rings a bell! They are on our radar! I had no idea they had a helicopter. I didn't think they could afford such a luxury!'

'They can't, not by selling their touristy bricks, pots, plates and lavatory chain handles! It's what's hidden inside some of their creations and packaging that make money, especially when shipped overseas!'

'Right, I follow that!'

'Good. Now this is important. With your boss's permission, I'd like you to bring Father John to the search area without his dog collar and clerical suit.'

'Not looking like a priest or monk?'

'Exactly. I want him to look like one of the search party – fluorescent jacket, baseball cap, hiker's trousers or even tracksuit bottoms. You get the idea? If you're late, we can start without him.'

'I'm sure we can deal with that – we've plenty of holiday-type clothing in the flat.'

'He needs to look nothing like he usually does, that's the message.'

'I don't know what you're up to, Mr Napier, but Gold Command won't want to get involved in something as low key as a hunt for a lost rambler.'

'You know the answer to that one. I'm relying on you to get your boss's approval.'

'I'll have to be open and say we're hoping to trap a drug dealer and multi-murderer. That should do the trick. Once Father John is suitably equipped, he'll join the search party and if anyone asks where he's from, all he has to say is that he's from Ashfordly and he's a volunteer. So in effect, he's looking for himself!'

'If you want to be invisible, Sue, the finest

way is to mingle with a crowd all wearing similar clothes and doing the same thing. Have you ever tried identifying one penguin from another?'

'I thought you wanted him to look and act like an old monk who's got dementia and who's lost? The idea being that the helicopter would "find" him?'

'I've changed my mind, that's too dangerous. It puts him at an unacceptable risk. Remember we're dealing with Goddard, a real villain.'

'What do you think he'll do? My boss will be interested.'

'Intelligence suggests that Goddard disposes of his victims by tossing them out of his helicopter. I think that's what happened to DI Radcliffe. Father John could be whisked away and dumped in the North Sea – dead. I can't risk that. And there's no time for rehearsals.'

'So who will we be looking for?'

'Me. I'll be armed with a handgun and dressed in a monk's habit, flitting in and out of the conifers away from the centre of activity so the helicopter will see me briefly whilst the main search party is diverted elsewhere. We've already had a reported sighting, so a monk flitting among the trees will really get things moving! I want the helicopter to see me whilst the main search party is diverted elsewhere.'

'I'm familiar with that patch of moorland. It's good hiking country. Shall I come in hiking gear?'

'Yes, be prepared to join the search party. I might need someone to see a fleeting figure and divert the others if they're getting too close.'

'I'll keep my mobile on.'

'Remember that our target – my target – is capable of anything and could have a gun, either in his 'copter or with him if he leaves. The 'copter could even be booby trapped if anyone tries to fly it – we must be aware of who we're dealing with, be wary of his reputation. Goddard, under various identities, stops at nothing; anyone in his way will be disposed of! We need our wits about us. Now, I'll give you a map reference for Gold Command – and I've alerted my chief constable. Can you take Father John to the scene, keep him under cover and in disguise until we're ready to infiltrate him into the search party? Don't let him know the truth, it would disturb him too much. He's done well so far.'

'He's been quite the actor with me!'

'It'll require a bit more play-acting but the main thing is that he's no longer the hunted monk with dementia. I am.'

'So you've netted Goddard?'

'Not yet, but I'm getting close.'

'I wish you the best of luck, Mr Napier.' She ended the conversation. 'I'll get things moving fast. See you on Whinstone Ridge.'

'I'll tell Inspector Carter what's going on. He needs to know a little more but not a lot.'

Napier left his office and spotted Detective Sergeant Salkeld as she strode through the murder room.

'Sarge,' he called to her. 'Can you add a team of firearms officers to the search? On the chief's authority – he's in touch with Gold Command. And I'll be armed too – officially. I'll brief the firearms officers when I arrive. Now I'm going to discuss something with Father Will in the cop shop. Has anything else happened that I should know about?'

'Just that we've got uniformed police officers already *en route* to Whinstone Ridge. They're being joined by more moorland rescue teams and two teams of police dogs with handlers.'

'Great, this is developing well but we've no time to waste. Any news about the target helicopter?'

'Nothing, it hasn't taken off yet.'

'Will you know when it does?'

'Yes, boss. Control room will inform me. I'll also be told when it lands near the old chapel to await a briefing by Inspector Carter.'

'Good. Keep in touch. Can you contact Friar Tuck straightaway and ask him to join

Father Will and me in the cop shop? I don't think he'll have gone up to join the search party just yet. Then I'll come back to see what's going on before we all head for the moors. Also I need a quiet chat with Inspector Carter.'

'Sir.'

When he arrived at the cop shop, Prior Tuck was already there.

'I want a chat with you both.' Napier glanced around the limited accommodation in the little police office. 'In confidence.'

'We can use my office,' suggested the prior.

'Secure, is it? From flapping ears and such?'

'Very,' the prior assured him.

'It might be a good idea if the abbot joined us – he should hear this.'

'I'll see if he's available.'

'Right, let's go.'

Abbot Merryman thought it wise that he should be fully aware of what was happening in his patch of England and joined the others. His office was at the far end of the upper corridor, only a few yards from the prior's. When everyone was settled, Napier took control. 'Thanks for coming, Father Abbot and everyone. I haven't much time but the world of crime fighting waits for no man. I'm about to join what appears to be a search for Father John. However, as you are all responsible in

280

some way for what happens here, you should have advance warning of my plans. First, and without going into detail, I can tell you that Father John is in safe hands.'

'What a relief!' sighed the abbot. 'So why the search?'

'Think back to yesterday morning. A murder victim was found in nearby woodland. He was an undercover police officer operating in the north of England on behalf of the London Metropolitan Police working in co-operation with Greater Manchester Police. Other parties involved are the Security Services, the Serious Organised Crime Agency and its undercover specialist drugs investigative officers. We have not yet released the victim's name or details of the murder.'

'Can I ask if you have linked that death with Father John's dilemma?' asked Abbot Merryman. 'He's not the killer, is he? Father John, I mean.'

'Fortunately, no! It's rather complicated but my first clues were the injuries to the deceased's body. I thought he had fallen or been pushed from the nearby cliff, then I realized his injuries were too serious for that. He was dead before he hit the ground, that was another clue, and it was when I heard someone had volunteered to search for Father John in a helicopter that I realized what had happened. Detective Inspector Radcliffe, the murder victim, had been killed elsewhere and I'm sure his body was tossed out of a helicopter. His injuries are consistent with a fall from a great height after death. That place in the woodland is upon a helicopter route that avoids the villages so the local people are accustomed to hearing them flying, their noise is not unusual, which is why no one reported suspicious helicopter noises. Now we have someone who is offering a helicopter to search for Father John.'

'He could be genuine,' suggested Prior Tuck.

'He could, but he isn't. Joe Morton, the man behind Linneymoor Ceramics, is a known drugs baron. I checked him out, as we say, not by normal CRO but by our secret files. His real name is Michael Goddard...'

'Now it's all beginning to make sense,' said Father Will. 'I never knew criminals could be so deceptive. Or rich! Goddard, the man who framed Father John!'

'I'm sure I heard something about our local murder on the radio,' said the abbot, frowning.

'Possibly. We announced that we're investigating the death but didn't give any details, neither did we confirm it was murder,' said Napier. 'However, on Saturday evening, Father Will stood in for his friend, Father John. During the confessions a woman arrived and spoke to Father Will who is bound by the seal of confession. I do not believe she was a Catholic or that she delivered a true confession but I do believe she thought she was speaking to Father John because his name was above the confessional – Father Will hadn't changed the name-board.'

The expression on Father Will's face indicated that he was still deeply upset by that encounter. None of the others at that meeting noticed the signs of grief.

'Father Will.' Napier lowered his voice a little. 'Without breaking the seal of confession, could you say your experience was enough to deeply unsettle you or perhaps any other priest who might have been in that confessional instead of you?'

The monk thought for a while, then nodded. 'Yes, definitely.'

'That's what was intended but it was not directed at you. It was a warning reinforced by the stiletto dagger in the confessional. A message and a warning – both intended for Father John. To unsettle him, frighten him. Even to get him accused of murdering the man in the woods by planting evidence. We know who was behind it – it was the gang who had killed the undercover policeman. Their trademark is death by a stiletto wound through the back of the neck – and that gang is led by Michael Goddard, now a highly successful drug dealer worth millions.'

'So why does he want rid of Father John?' asked the abbot.

'Some years ago, Goddard framed Father John for the murder of two little girls. Father John was then his neighbour and his name was John Jacobson. But since his release from prison, Father John has been working on his own cold-case review. He's gathered enough evidence to justify a cold-case review that will implicate Goddard.'

'I helped him.' Father Will spoke quietly. 'He has been steadily gathering evidence that will prove his innocence and I have spoken to him at length, and seen his files.'

'Now you know why Goddard, under whatever name he is now operating, wants to eliminate Father John – after making sure he is targeting the right person. Goddard discovered John had been released on licence and is now a monk here, but I guess he's not sure which one. Some time has passed since those murders. He looks much older and has a new identity. Goddard's highly efficient criminal network has almost traced Father John. I shall be there when he finally does.'

Abbot Merryman said, 'So what you're saying, Mr Napier, is that Goddard intends to eliminate Father John, whom he considers a real threat?'

'Yes, and there is also the revenge element because John discovered how drugs were being imported into prisons and he alerted the authorities. Goddard was prosecuted and his rich line of lucrative sales halted.'

'And Goddard's not the sort of man to sit back and do nothing!' commented Prior Tuck.

'Far from it. But in my view,' added Napier, 'he wants more than Father John's extinction – he must find and destroy the file that John has amassed. It will remain relevant even if John is not around to give evidence.'

'Father John must have been aware that he was in some kind of danger, heading off like he did on the pretext of a hospital appointment!' exclaimed Prior Tuck.

'Let's just say it has all been planned and he was made aware of the dangers but insisted on helping us. We'd received intelligence from Manchester to the effect that he was at serious risk. Certain high-class villains – if that's the right word – were out to get him – kill him, maim him, get revenge – and in time they discovered his new identity and where he was based. It was only a matter of time before they dealt with him. We had to make use of certain subterfuges to flush them out.'

'So you're saying that Father John's disappearance was a staged event?' puzzled the abbot.

'Yes, and it was made to look like the work of criminals to throw any local villainous informers off the scent. And we've located Goddard under a new identity, now manufacturing ceramics and living near Scar-

285

borough. Mission almost accomplished!'

'And now you are staging another event that involves poor Father John?'

'He'll be safe.' Napier sounded very confident. 'I'll see to that. I'll do all the dangerous stunts.'

'Then we shall all pray for him and for you!' said the abbot, smiling.

'The monkstables will be there to help,' added Prior Tuck, looking at his watch. 'They'll be there now. I felt I was more use here, staffing the cop shop.'

'We'll need all the help I can get, both here and there,' admitted Napier. 'Now I must go. I want to arrive after everyone else so can any of you find me a monk's habit with a hood? I need a very large one. I am going to be playing the part of an elderly senile monk who is lost on the moors. And I want Goddard to find me.'

Chapter 20

Napier, alone and in an unmarked police car, drove into the parking area and found a space among the search vehicles that had already arrived. He was dressed in his usual working clothes – a dark suit – but the monk's hooded habit, a large heavy garment, was in the boot.

He would head for the woodland before donning that. First, he needed a confidential word with Inspector Carter and called him on his mobile.

'Napier,' he introduced himself. 'I'm in the parking area, Inspector. A small grey car. Can you spare a couple of minutes? Here? Now? Just you and me.'

'Sir,' acknowledged the inspector.

Inspector Ray Carter, a sharp-featured man with a neat moustache, looked rather too small to be a police officer, which perhaps explained why he was such a good detective. Now a uniformed inspector, his usual duties meant he was in charge of Eltering sub-division. He was quickly at Napier's side and settled in the front passenger seat, dressed in hiking gear with an orange fluorescent jerkin bearing the legend 'POLICE SEARCH'.

'I won't keep you long, Inspector,' began Napier. 'But this is important, too important for flapping ears and the press to get hold of. First, though, how are things progressing?'

'Very well, sir. We've a good turn-out, everything from willing volunteers and your monk-constables to the Moorland Rescue Service and a team of hikers. We've around sixty or seventy searchers, I'd say. I've briefed them and some are already out there searching their allocated areas. There are a few press reporters too, and photographers. We're waiting for the police dogs and the firearms unit to arrive; they're coming from headquarters. It's a long drive but they should be here soon.'

'It all sounds promising. Is there any sign of the missing monk making use of the chapel, by the way?'

'It's difficult to say. It's often used by hikers who leave all sorts behind, but there's nothing in there looks very recent.'

'Good. So what about that ceramic chap with his helicopter? Any news of him?'

'No sign yet, sir. No word of take-off either.'

'He'll be checking things, making sure he's not been set up but he'll be here soon, you can bet on that,' said Napier with confidence. 'What about sightings of the missing monk? Any reports from the public hereabouts? The search has already featured on local radio.'

'Nothing, sir, not a whisper. I think that's very odd ... he must have gone to ground somewhere. We have the press here, local radio and TV news too, there'll be cameras and microphones everywhere.'

'That could be good for us. More people will come and join the search if it goes on for a long time, which it won't, I can assure you of that! Father John has not gone to ground so listen carefully.' Napier explained the situation as he outlined his plan, including the fact he would become the 'lost' monk clad in a black habit complete with a cowl. This was his plan because he wanted to arrest Joe Morton, the owner of the ceramics helicopter. He explained why, making sure the inspector realized exactly what sort of villains they would be dealing with, and provided their real identities.

'Do you know whether he's using a pilot or flying the thing himself?' he asked Carter.

'His wife is the pilot. But if he's as violent as you suggest, won't we need armed officers to deal with him?'

'I've arranged that, they'll be here soon and I'm armed. I need you to work out a feasible scheme to prevent Morton/Goddard's helicopter leaving the scene, especially if he succeeds in getting Father John on board by fair means or foul. That's the risk I'm taking. Now, in my guise as the fleeing monk, I will vanish into those trees like a wraith, only to surface somewhere in my highly recognizable monk's habit to ensure Goddard's helicopter sees me. Everyone will think I am the lost monk even if monks don't wear their cowls away from church or the abbey. When I am sighted, the helicopter will take to the air to locate me and monitor my movements. Then I'll hide until I can deal with them – with a little help from my friends, of course!'

'I'll look out for you too and direct it in the right direction.'

'Be sure you do that.'

'I will but if the 'copter belongs to who you say it does, surely he or the machine will be armed?'

'More than likely, Inspector. It might also be booby-trapped if we try to get into it without its owner's permission. I'm sure you realize that bombs can now be set off using mobile phones – that's something we'll have to worry about if it happens. We can't rehearse this, Inspector, but my gut feeling is that Goddard/Morton will be totally focused on capturing Father John alive. He has unfinished business with him – that's what all this is about. Our overriding concern is that he does not succeed in getting the monk on board his helicopter – he won't, because it will be me. But you now understand why I don't want him to find Father John.'

'I'm not quite sure what you're up to but I can do as I'm told. So where is Father John? Do you know?'

'He's on his way to join the search – to join those who are looking for him! He's got a minder with him, a capable security officer known as Sue, and she will dress him up as a searcher. She'll be armed but he'll join the others. No one will recognise him in his search gear – not many people know what he looks like anyway.'

'Does he really have to be here?'

'Unfortunately, he does. I need him to

identify Morton as the man he knew as Goddard, even if a few years have passed since they last met. Fingerprints will do that eventually but photographs are unreliable and can be doctored. In any case, I need to know immediately.'

'I think I've got all that. My job, then, is to make sure the searchers don't get their hands on you, even if you are spotted in the distance, but to allow the helicopter to get close but not close enough to whisk you on board and fly you away somewhere?'

'In a nutshell, yes. Of vital importance is the need to prevent the helicopter taking off afterwards, Inspector. I want to seize it as evidence. It could have drugs on board or merely an empty secret compartment for them. If so, it will bear traces that can be found. I need that evidence if I'm to nail this man. I want the helicopter flown to the forensic lab to be examined for blood too – the blood of Detective Inspector Radcliffe in particular. I believe his body and others were pushed out of it, some perhaps into the sea. If so, there must be some evidence of their presence despite being cleaned – blood or DNA. I have a qualified pilot standing by – her name is Sue. What we do not want is Morton to take off and disappear into the wide blue yonder. We might never see him or his helicopter again. Remember he's got a double murder charge to answer at the very least, not to mention a stack of drugs offences.'

'If he has a pilot fired up and ready, we might have problems.'

'Problems are to make us think, Inspector, not to worry. Now, Sue and Father John will be here soon. First, I'll get them to rendez-vous with me in the car park, then she'll bring him to you. Both will be dressed as volunteer searchers. Let them join other search parties but don't let them wander away on their own, they'll stand out like sore thumbs. They must merge into the back-ground – Morton won't be looking for them, he'll have his eyes open for a monk in distress, not a man like me who is capable of defending himself! We'll keep in touch on our mobiles.'

'Sssh!' Inspector Carter held his finger up. 'Helicopter! I can hear it in the distance, heading this way.'

'I won't appear in my monk's robes just yet, Inspector. When the 'copter lands, say you've had a sighting of the monk in Eagle Wood, that's half a mile south from here, just over that brow. When I'm ready, I'll call you and that's the time to send a few searchers in that general direction before the 'copter lands – it will make things look authentic. I'll go as well, but not in the cowl – I'll carry my habit and turn into a monk once I'm among those trees. Then I'll let the helicopter get a glimpse of me. This is going to be fun...'

'I'd hardly call it that!'

'Then let's refer to it as Exercise Phoenix.'

Chapter 21

Sue persuaded Father John to remain out of sight until the briefing was over; she did not want any of the monkstables or anyone else recognizing him, particularly passengers in the incoming helicopter that sounded very close. A few moments later, it appeared from behind distant trees, a handsome Robinson R44 in the cream and terracotta livery of Linneymoor Ceramics. As everyone watched its noisy approach, Napier took the opportunity to slip away, using whins and conifers as cover as he made for the dense woodland over which the helicopter had just flown.

All attention was upon the aircraft as it touched down on a piece of smooth ground a hundred yards or so from the chapel, sending up clouds of dust and debris as its rotors slowly came to a halt, watched by a crowd of eager searchers gathered for their briefing. Some were carrying hiking sticks, others had brought their dogs and most had well-filled backpacks in the event of a protracted search. Many volunteers were members of experienced search organizations such as Moorland Search and Rescue, or the National Park team. The uniformed monkstables were there too as were teams from the county police and other organizations – even the Young Farmers had sent a team of three sturdy young men. Two local doctors with experience of moorland searches had also volunteered.

From his vantage point on the stretch of elevated ground near the old chapel, Inspector Carter watched events, seeing that Napier had now disappeared into the distant woodland and that Father John was out of sight and awaiting his role in this curious affair. Carter felt it was all rather over the top, much more than a search for a missing monk, but he had faith in Napier's actions.

The engine of the Ceramics helicopter was switched off and the rotors almost halted before its crew prepared to disembark. The pilot was a woman but both she and her male companion were dressed in flying suits fashioned in the colours of their aircraft.

As the rotors reduced their spinning to almost a standstill, the couple ducked out of their doors and made their way towards the crowd. Inspector Carter raised a hand in greeting – the crowd blocked his way towards meeting them and so he was unable at that stage to bid them a welcome. Having acknowledged Mr and Mrs Morton, he would speak to them after the briefing.

With help from the leader of the Moorland Search and Rescue, each group leader, and the helicopter crew, were issued with local large-scale maps. All were able to read them and from these it was clear that the moorland and woods around Whinstone Ridge had been divided into individual search areas, each allocated to a leader with his or her team. Gathering them into a group in front of the chapel and addressing them by standing on an old chair, Inspector Carter first introduced himself and then explained their role, providing a brief description of the man they were seeking – a monk in his sixties, grey haired and about six feet tall. He was thought to be dressed in a monk's black habit with a cowl.

'His name is Father John and he should not be hard to find. If you do find him, bring him here if he is capable of walking or call one of our doctors who will go to him. We can arrange a stretcher party if necessary. I shall remain here where I have the mobile phone numbers of all search leaders and doctors. I'm also in radio contact with Gold Command and all the local emergency services who are aware of this search and standing by. Representatives of the media are also here. If you find Father John, please bring him to this chapel; it would be helpful for him and everyone involved. If you see him running off to hide or find any evidence of his presence, don't keep the details to yourselves. Tell me and I will divert others to help you. This is our centre of operations where you'll find me. I will be here most of the time if you need to speak to me. There are some ancient pews inside and a primitive outside toilet at the rear. Don't be afraid to take a break and rest if you need to – we don't want more casualties!'

They were reminded that Father John had been missing since Saturday but whether he had sheltered in the old chapel was not known. It did raise the question of whether he could have survived without cover on these heights on a chill autumn night. If he was still alive, he could be in a very poor state, perhaps due to exposure and a lack of food. He might be suffering from hypothermia, complete fatigue or something worse. Carter followed with advice about the terrain they were to search and general advice for any newcomers, reminding them that a helicopter would also be searching and in radio contact. The volunteers began to filter away in a very orderly manner, moving slowly in a long line, side by side, heading from west to east as, with sticks, they examined every patch of heather, whin, undergrowth and eventually the coniferous woodland.

The broad guidelines did not affect the helicopter – it would cover the immense open space with ease, hopefully guiding searchers towards their target if he was spotted. Press photographers and TV cameras had arrived and were in action, whilst among them were two police photographers, indistinguishable from their media counterparts. Their presence was for a totally different purpose – after all, this was a trap for a cold-blooded killer even though most of the searchers – and many police officers – were unaware of that.

As the large group of volunteers spread out, Mr and Mrs Morton remained at the back of the crowd but then approached Inspector Carter. So this grey-haired man and blonde-dyed woman in smart flying suits were the infamous Michael and Geraldine Goddard? They did not look at all like drug dealers, murderers or villains – even now, were being regarded as benefactors to the community! Inspector Carter decided to treat them with feigned respect as, in his guise as Joe Morton, the man took the lead.

'You're Inspector Carter, I heard you say. I'm Joe Morton, this is my wife, Rachel. Linneymoor Ceramics. You're expecting us, I believe?'

'We are, and it's good of you to help us like this.'

'No problem,' responded the man with a faint Lancashire accent. 'I heard your briefing so where do you want us?'

Inspector Carter handed him a copy of the map that had been issued to the other searchers. 'You can see how the search parties are spreading out so I think a sweep of this particular part of the moorland, as far as we can see from here and beyond, needs to be searched from the air. I think that will be a good place to start.'

'What's the procedure if we spot him? We might not be able to land nearby.'

'You should contact me on this mobile number,' advised the inspector, handing him a card. 'We will direct a ground team to the scene to assess the situation and probably help the monk to your machine to be brought to shelter.'

'So if it's possible for us to land near him, and if I see that he needs urgent hospital treatment, can I take him directly to hospital? That would make sense. Speed is of the essence...'

'That's a welcome offer, Mr Morton, but let's deal with that if and when it occurs,' said Inspector Carter as several photographers, including those from the police, took photographs. 'Our immediate priority is to find him, then assess his physical condition.'

'Point taken. So where was the last sighting?'

'It was rather vague, a call from a hiker who didn't want to be identified – dodging off work with a woman who wasn't his wife! He'd seen our target near this old chapel but failed to give more precise information.'

'Obviously he provided some useful information otherwise we'd not be here?'

'From what he told us, this is our starting point, and now centre of operations. Apparently he wandered aimlessly close to the woodland but that was some time ago. He has been missing since Saturday but if he's still able to walk, he could be anywhere. He might be in that wood, lying hidden perhaps. Ill or injured.'

'So it's anyone's guess where he might be?'

'If he's hiding, he might be in that woodland. Have you any experience at searching woodland?'

'Not a lot, I must admit. It's not the easiest of jobs when airborne but not impossible – often there are open patches, tracks running through and so on. We can only do our best. What do you think, Rachel?'

'We came here to do a job, Joe. We know what's required. We should get started right away – don't forget a life is at stake.'

'Does that fit your plans, Inspector?'

'It's fine, there's no time to lose.'

'I'll fly over this open section of moorland and then towards those woods,' announced Rachel. 'I can cope with the wooded areas and we can always guide searchers on the ground if we spot him...'

'Right, sounds fine to me,' said Inspector Carter.

'Rachel's the pilot and I'm the observer today, but before I go, I need the loo,' announced Joe. 'You said there's one behind the chapel – I can't cope with this suit! How about you, love?'

'I'm fine,' said Rachel. 'See you back at Crusoe.'

'Crusoe?' queried the inspector.

'After Robinson, our machine's a Robinson R44. Four seater, that is. Like him, I suppose you could say we're looking for footprints in the sand today.'

'I need the toilet,' whispered Father John to Sue, both dressed in their hooded outfits with POLICE SEARCH emblazoned their backs. They had followed and mingled with the crowd for only a short time but no one had talked to them.

'It's urgent,' John pressed her. 'It's my prostate cancer. When you've got to go, you've got to go. It's a bit open here, no trees...'

'I'm not supposed to let you out of my sight like this but the inspector said there's a loo behind the chapel. Don't be long. I'll wait here. We can catch up with the others.'

Sue watched as the search party left her

behind. It was now divided into several groups, each with a leader, and they were making their first tentative steps in what already had all the appearances of a major hunt. She waited as Father John disappeared behind the bulk of the old chapel. At that point, she lost sight of him.

As Father John hurried about his urgent business, he saw a man in a flying suit heading in the opposite direction to the other searchers as he also hurried towards the stone toilet at the rear of the chapel. It was the man from Linneymoor Ceramics with his smart helicopter, here to help in the search. In this situation, Father John wondered how the man would cope with his flying suit. He might find out because it was a sure bet they'd arrive together – so would there be more than one stall in there? He sincerely hoped so.

They arrived together from opposite directions and John, being a polite monk, stood back to allow the other first entry. But the man stopped and at that instant John recognized him despite the passage of time. He said nothing, doing his best to conceal his surprise and horror at the situation in which he now found himself. Alone with Michael Goddard...

And Goddard recognized him.

'I've been looking for you, John. All these years. You're coming with me, very peacefully and very quietly, for a ride in my smart new helicopter...'

'No, no, I can't...'

'This says you can and you will.' Goddard pulled a tiny handgun from a pocket in his flying suit. 'Nobody is going to see us, nobody is going to see you. I need you alive for a little longer then you will disappear for ever. These people will never find you. But first we have a little job to do, both of us... After you...' And he stood in the narrow doorway to block any attempted escape by Father John.

Chapter 22

To reach the security of the helicopter with his captive, Goddard had to pass the western end of the chapel, then cross a wide empty space. Its surface was anything but smooth or level – it was a patch of rough moorland covered with stones, heather and stubbly scrub plants. Some rescuers were searching nearby but paid no attention to the two men emerging from the toilet. Goddard hissed at Father John, warning him not to draw attention to himself. The gun pressing on his ribs persuaded John to remain calm even if he was trembling with fear. They walked side by side, apparently chatting amiably about some forthcoming action, and the illusion was strengthened because John was dressed as one of the searchers. Napier's hastily arranged plan had had an unforeseen outcome, the complete opposite of what he'd intended. But Goddard was no fool – he realized in an instant that he had fallen into a clever trap. John had not been wandering or lost, he was here, up front and in disguise. He was the bait and it was time to leave. John had become his guarantee of freedom and so Goddard would ensure they walked closely together, side by side, looking like colleagues or friends.

'Rachel' had noticed the pair walking towards her and it took a few moments for her to realize that this was indeed the John they were seeking. So why all these searchers? Something odd was going on. She knew her husband would be holding a handgun that would be invisible to casual observers while pressed into John's side. Goddard would take no chances – the pistol would be loaded. Such behaviour had become increasingly common in recent years when he'd had to deal with those who had sought to undermine or control his business empire.

Right now, he seemed to be coping easily with his captive so she hurried ahead to open the helicopter doors. Michael/Joe would not linger one second longer than necessary –

after the useful if brief publicity surrounding their arrival, they could now depart with honour, claiming an urgent and unexpected family commitment. For them, the search was over.

All the others were concentrating upon their own tasks and no one seemed to notice Father John making his slow progress towards the helicopter. But Sue was acutely observant. Just as she realized John was rather late emerging from the toilet, she noticed the pair walking close together, with the older man sometimes stumbling. Instantly she knew Father John had been trapped and that meant his certain death. On her mobile, she alerted Napier, who was hidden in the nearby woodland awaiting his dramatic role.

'How in the name of God did that happen?' he bellowed. 'Get Carter! Tell him to do something. Alert the firearms unit. We have to stop the helicopter taking off, stop them getting Father John on board. If they succeed, he's a gonner. Look out for guns … these people are dangerous villains, very dangerous … I'm on my way.' And his phone went dead.

Sue was unknown to everyone except Father John, and almost anonymous in her searcher's outfit. She hurried across the expanse of heather to where uniformed constables in white helmets were combing the moorland. She was not to know they were monkstables. She reached them without attracting undue attention; she appeared to be a rescuer going for an urgent chat with a police team.

'Is Inspector Carter here?'

'Not with us, he's with the firearms unit, over there,' replied the uniformed monk, pointing to the inspector.

'Who's in charge here?' she demanded.

'Me. Prior Tuck and the monk-constables of Maddleskirk Abbey at your service.' And he raised his white helmet. 'How can we help?'

'Monks? As policemen? Specials, are you?'

'No, we're professionals from Maddleskirk Abbey. We're fully trained so how can we help?'

'I'm not quite sure but it is urgent ... deadly urgent ... that man over there.'

She pointed to Goddard and John. 'That man is your Father John and he is being led at gunpoint into that helicopter. He's got to be stopped. Chief Superintendent Napier has ordered us to prevent him being taken inside and we have to prevent the helicopter taking off...'

'By us, you mean?' asked Prior Tuck, somewhat shocked. 'So who are you?'

'My name is Sue, I've been looking after Father John. There's no one else here right now and we've only got seconds ... it's vital we stop the 'copter taking off.' And she produced a small pistol from her clothing.

'But how does Father John come to be here?'

'There's no time for questions, Prior Tuck. John's in great danger – action is needed now! And I mean right now before that thing starts its props and gets airborne! And the kidnapper is armed. We must stop him...'

'Say no more!' Prior Tuck sprang into action, his police experience coming to the fore as he found himself imagining he'd jumped into deep water with no knowledge of how to swim. He'd have to work things out as they progressed. 'Who's got the gun?' he asked. 'What sort is it?'

'The man with Father John. He's Goddard, he's got a handgun of some kind, a small pistol.' She pointed. 'You can't see it but it's there...'

'I'll call the monkstables, they're all here.' He produced a police whistle from his tunic and blew hard. It worked. They all turned to stare in his direction and he shouted as he waved his arms. 'Here! Now!' He blew it two more times. The trouble was, it also alerted Father John's captor.

'Run, damn you, run!' shouted Goddard, prodding John with his pistol.

But John's legs seemed to give way. He was almost on his knees as Goddard tried to bundle him towards the helicopter, still many yards away. As one, the monkstables started to run; his whistle had also alerted other searchers who followed the example of the monkstables and began to move towards him, if a little slowly and with some uncertainty before increasing their pace. The good old-fashioned police whistle could still produce results! The helicopter should soon be surrounded.

'That's impressive,' she breathed. 'Are they all monks?'

'Those in uniform, yes, but trained as policemen. And I used to be in the regular force.' The seven monkstables of Maddleskirk Abbey and a crowd of searchers arrived together. Prior Tuck addressed them. 'We must make sure that helicopter remains grounded but the man on the left has a gun. It's a handgun which means you couldn't hit a barn door with it if you sat on the sneck but if he fires at random he might get in a lucky shot. If we run towards him, zig-zagging as we go, he won't know how to stop us, except he might attempt a lucky shot.'

He paused momentarily to allow his words to have an effect, then continued, 'Pray hard he misses! It's the man in the search gear who's at risk ... let's hope his captor doesn't loose a shot into him but I think he's too valuable to lose. Let's go.'

With the monkstables and searchers closing the gap, Goddard was struggling to force Father John into a faster pace. Father

John kept letting his knees collapse so that he fell to the ground or else stumbled every few yards, playing for time as he realized he must never board this helicopter. 'Come on, come on, come on!' shouted Goddard. 'Get up ... you'll be safe with me, John...'

As he struggled with John's apparent incapacity to move any further or any faster, Goddard noticed his wife racing across the heather, intent on gaining the pilot's seat as the group of uniformed police officers closed in. Neither he nor she realized they were monks.

As they all stampeded towards the helicopter, they were encouraged by a lot of very loud shouting from a huge monk in a cowl who was bellowing, 'Stop it taking off! Stop it! It must be stopped!' as he led his troops. 'Look out for guns! You, the armed police, take the lead, get that couple in your sights, disable them, stop them shooting us or John...'

Police officers, a few carrying loaded rifles, realized the shouting monk was the mighty Detective Chief Superintendent Napier in disguise, his monk's habit flapping as he bellowed, 'Stop them, stop them!'

But these cavalry-like reinforcements, with armed police officers among them, still had a distance to travel before they became effective. It was the monkstables who were ahead and leading the charge. The pilot was now aboard and she started the rotor blades to allow them to build up speed once her husband and his captive had clambered inside. And all the time, the monkstables were gaining valuable ground.

'Drape yourselves across the boom!' shouted Prior Tuck, panting as he galloped ever forward. 'That's the long slender bit that sticks out at the back, with the little propeller on the end. The 'copter can't take off with a large weight on there ... and the rest of you – everybody – do likewise. Drape yourselves across its tail, that'll ground it...'

'No! Don't do that!' bellowed Napier who had caught up to the others and arrived with giant strides in his thick black habit. 'Those blades will rip your heads off. The 'copter will keel over ... keep clear ... it's too bloody dangerous ... back off...'

And so they did, halting their onward gallop.

'He's coming with me or he dies!' shrieked Goddard, hauling Father John to his feet yet again. This time he ducked beneath John's limp body and hoisted him upon his shoulders, his arms effectively immobilizing John's legs and arms. It was a swift and well-executed manoeuvre as John was carried over the final few yards towards the open door of the helicopter and unceremoniously dumped inside. Goddard clambered in after him and closed the door. The pilot was in her seat ready for lift-off. With Father John struggling weakly as the pistol, still in Goddard's fist, was mere inches from his face, the rotor blades gained momentum as their tips rose higher into the air with their ear-aching throbbing, chopping sound.

The tail rotor was spinning to give stability to the machine as it prepared for take-off from its pair of long skis.

'I want them all alive!' shouted Napier to anyone within earshot as the pitch of the engines and the throb of the rotors drowned all other sounds. 'Don't shoot now but keep your weapons cocked and ready to fire. Everyone...'

Everything seemed to be happening in slow motion and it appeared that Napier had capitulated – but then he broke into a short and rapid sprint as he stripped off the heavy black habit and ran to the rear of the helicopter. Standing as close as possible to the whirling tail rotor as he could, he flung the habit over the blades and within a fraction of a second, the thick fabric became entangled with the blades and the prop shaft, literally smothering the rotary motion. It was now impossible for the helicopter to take off. He'd learned that trick from a helicopter pilot.

'Firearms unit, take aim. Cover the pilot and crew ... Father Mutch Miller, you're the strong man of the monkstables, get John out of that cab ... fast as you can ... we'll cover you!' shouted Napier.

As Father Mutch made his way towards the passenger door under the protection of rifle cover, Napier shouted, 'One of you cover the pilot. Mrs Goddard, leave that machine. Now!'

She had to await the gradual wind-down of the rotors, with the helicopter disabled in a strange silence.

'Out!' snapped Napier, who opened her door when it was safe. 'Cover her every move,' he directed his armed officers and she cautiously left the aircraft.

Napier addressed Goddard. 'Now you, Goddard, drop your gun and put your hands on your head, NOW! Do it now, or you get a bullet ... raise your arms above your head. You're both nicked.'

Without taking his eyes off the pair, Napier shouted, 'Everyone else – get as far back as possible and lie flat on the ground ... everybody ... NOW! This machine might be booby-trapped ... it might explode...'

Father Mutch had managed to manhandle John out of the helicopter and was running with him at his side, heading as far away as possible before lying on the ground behind a hummock. When the pilot was safe from the rotors, Mrs Goddard obeyed Napier's orders, a marksman having her in his sights.

He had a good view as she descended from the cockpit and covered her every step. She appeared to be in a desperate hurry.

'Over here!' called the officer with a rifle. 'Now!'

She obeyed, then Sue frisked her for concealed weapons; there was none, no stiletto, no firearm. The policeman produced a set of handcuffs and locked her wrists behind her back.

'Can I go now?'

'We've a vehicle waiting,' said the police officer.

'I want to get away from here...'

'You're going nowhere!'

While almost all eyes had been on the pilot, Goddard had emerged from the 'copter under the close watch of an armed policeman. His hands were clasped together on top of his head. He was walking from the helicopter as Napier eased himself closer to the firearms officer, who had his rifle aimed at Goddard's moving head. 'We need him alive,' he whispered to the officer. 'He's got something in his hand, look. Right hand. On his head ... it looks like a mobile ... bring him down, shoot him in the leg, the knees if you can. I'll stage a diversion.'

For the briefest of moments, no one moved.

Then Napier shouted, 'I'll walk towards Goddard with an offer he can't refuse. Keep your eyes on whatever he's clutching on his head...'

There was silence as everyone stopped to watch this drama.

'Goddard!' shouted Napier. 'I'm coming to talk to you, I'm sure we can discuss this like civilized men. I am not armed.' He began his lonely, dangerous walk, arms raised above his head.

'Keep away, keep away, keep away!' shrieked Goddard. 'Keep away, I said!'

He waved his right hand and Napier saw he was still clutching the gadget that looked like a mobile phone. Immediately two shots rang out as Goddard sank to the ground with both knees broken, the device spinning away from him.

'Get me away from here!' he screamed.

'Run!' shouted Napier at Father John, then he bellowed, 'Everybody stay down ... cover your heads...'

Napier managed to gallop about twenty yards from the helicopter as it exploded in a fireball which produced a huge cloud of black smoke and sent metal splinters and other debris flying in all directions. The blaze crackled and produced lots more minor explosions as the searchers dropped to the ground for safety or hid behind boulders. Many of them witnessed Goddard's instant death from a piece of flying jagged metal that hit him in the neck whilst he lay immobile.

His wife, still handcuffed, tried to flee but there was a police officer in pursuit; a rugby tackle brought her to the ground as she had been heading for shelter in a small clump of conifers.

'We've got her but he had that coming to him, I can't mourn him,' commented Napier, 'but it's his wife I want to talk to. I think she's the brains behind all this ... but well done, everyone.'

After the initial explosion, the stricken helicopter settled down to be consumed by the fire that was now raging through it, fanned by the moorland breeze and as things calmed down, Napier was first to move. He was heading towards the stricken helicopter when it suddenly exploded again with a plume of dark smoke rising from the flames that wrapped its carcase; he hurled himself to the ground as the fire roared, then it stopped as suddenly as it had started. There were no further casualties but it was another half-hour before anyone could approach the blackened remains of the helicopter.

'Somebody will have to clear up this mess,' shouted Napier as people became mobile once more. 'But not until we've got the evidence we need.'

At that point, a small blue Morris traveller arrived and out stepped ex-Sergeant Oscar Blaketon and ex-PC Ventress.

'You left it a bit late!' shouted Napier.

'We've got him!'

'I shall pray for his soul,' offered Prior Tuck.

'I won't,' said Napier.

And so the siege of Whinstone Ridge ended without further loss of life. The remains of the helicopter, which included a surviving cache of drugs destined for delivery later that day, were eventually removed on a low loader for forensic examination. Its shattered car-case contained the DNA from Detective Inspector Radcliffe, in addition to evidence of other murders, serious crimes and drugs offences. Goddard's body was eventually removed to the mortuary for a post-mortem and Napier called for a loud-hailer to thank everyone.

Geraldine Goddard was sentenced to twenty-five years' imprisonment as an accessory to the murder of Inspector Radcliffe, and a cold-case review was opened into the murder of the Goddard girls. It was belatedly revealed that Goddard did have a motive for their murder – their natural father was a drugs baron who had warned Goddard off his pitch and stolen some of his most valuable customers. The killings were Goddard's brutal revenge on his rival; they brought that bloodline to an end.

Scientific tests established the innocence of the man now known as Father John and confirmed the guilt of Michael Goddard, not for one murder but several, in addition to innumerable drugs offences. The woman called Sue disappeared as suddenly as she had arrived.

Father John remained peacefully in Maddleskirk Abbey whilst Detective Chief Superintendent Napier became a frequent visitor to the abbey church to listen to the monks chanting their calming music. 'I'll be back,' he said to the abbot on one such occasion as the monkstables continued to preserve the tranquillity of their monastery. 'But hopefully in peace and not to deal with another murder.'

'Amen to that,' said Abbot Merryman.

The publishers hope that this book has given you enjoyable reading. Large Print Books are especially designed to be as easy to see and hold as possible. If you wish a complete list of our books please ask at your local library or write directly to:

Magna Large Print Books
Magna House, Long Preston,
Skipton, North Yorkshire.
BD23 4ND